THE ROOM

ROGUE BOOKS

Cover design by Ryan Bibby of Novel Branding. You can contact Mr. Bibby at ryan.a.bibby@gmail.com.

Special thanks to Judith Schwartz of FinalEyes Copyediting for her remarkable editing and attention to detail.

Follow Derek on Facebook, Twitter (@DerekBlass), and his blog on Wordpress

Visit the fun, flash website for Rogue Books at www.rogue-books.com

ISBN: 978-0-9855492-1-3

Printed in the United States of America

THE ROOM

DEREK BLASS

ROGUE BOOKS
DENVER

To Itzel

ONE

The twins were playing in the basement when the first box arrived. Grown, sweating men steadily brought cardboard boxes full of their lives down to them, creating brown columns that the girls played around. First, they were the columns of a great estate. Then, they were the columns of a dungeon. Then, they were columns supporting the whole world above them.

Don supervised that world above them, checking on the girls with a call down the steps every ten minutes or so. Faith set to pouncing on the boxes, reading the labels she had meticulously affixed to each one. Then, like a master hunter, she gutted the contents and rapidly put things in their rightful places.

"You know, I can help you unload all that," Don said to her.

Breathlessly, she replied, "Just keep the flow coming."

The flow was important. The flow didn't exist at their home in Seattle, where their movers damaged half of their wedding china and unceremoniously backed over a box of the girls' favorite toys. He recalled kneeling in the rain and trying to shove stuffed animals back into the box before the next wave of traffic came. With a smile, Don returned to his post, watched each box come out and made sure each one was safely escorted into its new home.

"New" as in new to them. Very old to this world. 1929, to be exact. A Tudor only six miles from the thriving downtown. Five stories in all, from top to bottom. It was a deceptively large house that suited Don and Faith's downplayed good fortune, and represented the culmination of an arduous eight months of search. The house search was a relentless process led by Don's tendency to over-analyze and Faith's refusal to settle. The process nearly alienated their realtor.

When they saw this house however, every other option disappeared. Love masked the house's warts, which were many. The house was abandoned by its former owner, left in disrepair, stripped even of its switch plates and overhead lights. The yards were all weeds and dirt, and stood out from the surrounding homes like a meth addict in a choir group. Challenge — sometimes the fool's gold of life — overcame Don and Faith. This beat-down relic would be their multiyear project.

The bottom level was a basement, completely below grade, consisting of a big room with a butler's pantry. To the left of the stairs was a hallway that led to another bedroom on the right, and then a laundry room with an exterior staircase to the ground level. The basement, like the entire house, was filthy. On the floor was an old white carpet, stained a toxic brown and green. The lath and plaster was deteriorating at various locations where water flooded the house when the pipes froze over last winter. Windows had various panes in their lead frames broken out — the product of local vagrants.

The next level up was a garden level, half a level above the basement, and half a level below the ground outside. A small bathroom was walled off on that level. Its cast iron tub was rimmed around the bottom with black scum. Bright orange paint adorned certain parts of the walls. An outdated pedestal sink stood next to where it should have been connected to water lines The rest of the garden-level room was light brown under a cheap piece of wood trim, and white above that except on one long wall painted a cheap blue. The floor was half covered by a wood laminate that the prior owner had started. The rest of the floor was exposed concrete covered with plastic.

"Don!"

He heard the call from outside and responded from the front door. "Yeah?"

"I found your baseball cards!"

He smiled. It was one of the boxes they couldn't track after closing the door to their old house for the last time. A box containing all the baseball cards collected since he was a child. He went inside and found Faith squatting over it, obviously perplexed about where its contents would go. This was unexpected, and for Faith a surprise that she didn't necessarily welcome with open arms. Don knew she already had places scouted out for all of the boxes' cargo.

"That makes me happy. The girls still downstairs?" She nodded. "I don't like them down there that much. Kinda dangerous."

She rolled her eyes and then broke her focus to glance at him. "It's dangerous *everywhere* in this house, Donald."

The statement conveyed more than the obvious truth, about which it was accurate. It conveyed the unspoken fact that the condition of the house was to be his duty, and all bad things associated with the condition attached to him. A veteran of the battles of marriage, he bit his tongue and returned to supervision of the moving crew.

Several hours later they were seated around a makeshift dining room of box seats and a coffee table. McDonald's wrappers littered the area. The twins asked if they could return to playing. Exhausted, Don assented and gathered the trash from the meal.

"It was a blessing to have twins," Dan mused.

Faith snorted. "Did you push them out of you?"

Dan shrugged his shoulders. "I didn't say that part was easy, but they've got playmates for life. That part is great."

Faith came over with a box cutter in her hand. "You've got more work to do, mister."

"You're a real slave driver." Faith tried to give him a hug, but a scream from the girls tore through the house. Don spun around and bolted up the steps from the main level. Another scream situated the girls on the bedroom level. He slid into the pink room on the hardwood floors. This room would belong to the girls. They were standing over something at the back corner of the room.

"Girls, what is it?" They backed up together and then split apart. Don moved in. He leaned down and saw a tiny mouse, eyes missing, its skin sucked into its skeleton. He grabbed it by the tail and swung it around just as he knew Faith was coming in. She gasped and jumped back.

"You jerk!"

"Yeah, Dad, you jerk!" the girls cried in unison.

He grinned, pleased with himself, and flushed the mouse down the only operating toilet in the house.

* * * * *

It was Monday, and Don was gone at the new law firm where he be vaulted away billing legal hours. The girls played in the backyard. Faith grabbed the box labeled "China" and trudged back up to the main level. This level was open, one of the prior owners having blown out all the walls. A fireplace dominated the entry area. Moving across the level, there was a room that served as a seating area, and then a semicircular room they would use as their dining area. At least, that's how Faith envisioned it after they finished everything.

She set the box down and cut it open. Each piece of china was wrapped in newspaper and then bubble wrap. It upset her beyond belief that movers destroyed half of their wedding set. She set out the remaining pieces and the mish-mash depressed her even more. "Not even four matched place settings."

The doorbell rang and jolted her. She was sitting right next to the chimes hanging from a mahogany cabinet on the wall. The things could knock the fillings out of a person's mouth. She went to the front door and opened the antique peephole to scan the stoop. No one there. Another knock on the door. Faith furrowed her eyebrows and stood on her tiptoes to get a better view. A child looked up at her.

"New to the neighborhood, right?"

Faith smiled at the child. How odd that he would be so direct. "We are." She opened the door and he stood there, unmoving, with a tin foil-wrapped plate in his hands.

"I made this for you," he said, holding the plate out.

5

"Well, come on in." Faith went to take a step back, but realized that her twins were hanging onto her legs.

"No, I better not." Faith tilted her head at him. He handed the plate to Brooke, the gutsier of the twins.

Brooke glanced at Faith to get final approval. When Faith didn't object, she spoke. "Thank you."

The little boy walked off without saying another word.

"Strange," Faith muttered to herself. She shut the door and turned the hammered nickel deadbolt.

"Mommy, who was that?" Charity asked.

"A kind neighbor."

"He was weird."

Faith ran her hand through Charity's hair. "Maybe just a little bit nervous."

"Well, he left a cherry pie," Brooke gleamed. "And, I'm going to have some of it!" She took off to the kitchen.

"Hold on!" Faith called out. "I want to look at that first." She inspected the pie on the kitchen counter, breaking off a piece of the crust and smelling it. All looked normal. Brooke danced around the kitchen, singing "the pie is mine." She stopped and grinned when she noticed Faith watching. "Go on, get a knife out of the drawer."

Faith made some progress over the next few hours with the boxes, which seemed to multiply like mercury hit by a hammer. The girls were content to help every hour or so, taking breaks from their adventures to grab a fruit juice and haphazardly throwing the contents of some box into closets or onto shelves. The day wore on in that manner until Faith heard the beep of the alarm system. Don was back, and just in time for the girls to erupt into a fight.

"It's mine!"

"No, it's mine!" Charity screamed back. The knowledge that without outside assistance she would lose this battle to Brooke was visible on her face. Just like she always lost. They were twins, but distinct in every respect except for physical appearance.

"Girls, girls. What the heck are you fighting over?" Don leaned on the front door to close it and mentally added a sticky door jamb to the list of things to fix. The girls stopped for a moment. Don looked over at Faith who was crouched over a box like a crab, shaking her head. The last thread connecting her mind to sanity was often visible, and the girls plucked at it every day.

"Listen, girls. You see that woman over there? Remember what she does to bad kids." He paused to note the amusement spread on their faces. "You remember, right?"

The girls dropped their arms. Charity was the one still holding the object. Brooke came over and cupped her hand over his ear. He nodded his head as she spoke, keeping an eye trained on Faith. The grin on her face revealed that she knew what was coming.

"That's right, Brooke. The *witch* puts bad little kids into the

7

cauldron for cooking. See her? She looks hungry, don't you think?"

Faith burst into laughter. "Cut that out!"

Don smiled and looked at Charity. "You mind if I take a peek at that?"

She shook her head with the gentleness that separated her from everyone else in the house. The rest of them had an edge, whether it be wit or cunning or ambition. That was always a source of late-night, right-before-sleep speculation between Faith and Don. How did she end up the *only* truly sweet person in the house?

He took the object. It was a grisly stuffed doll, dirty to the point of being a singular gray color. Stitches cut across the doll's stomach. It had one eye left, and just an ill-formed mouth. The thing immediately gave him the chills.

"Where did you two find this?" Faith noted the tone in his voice and came over to inspect the doll for herself.

"Basement bedroom," the twins responded.

Don scratched the back of his head and looked at Faith. She grabbed the reins. "I'm going to toss this into one of these empty boxes," she said, "and you're going to forget it existed, okay?" The girls nodded. "You've got so many nice, new toys. Why do you have to play with something like this?"

"All our toys are in boxes!"

Don shrugged his shoulders. "They've got a point." He went

over to one of the caches of boxes and rooted around until he found a box marked "Girls' Toys." With a car key he was able to slice open the tape sealing it shut. "Have at it!"

He stepped aside and went back over to Faith to find her lips for a quick kiss. Suit jacket in hand, he shuffled through the mail on the counter.

"Anything other than junk mail yet?" he asked instinctively.

"Not yet," Faith responded. "Probably not for a while." She leaned into him and lowered her voice. "What the heck do you think that thing is?"

"What thing?" he answered absentmindedly while tossing envelopes into the trash.

"That doll."

He turned his attention to her. "Well, just that. A doll."

She pinched him on the arm. "I saw your face, Donald. I saw your face."

"It's a doll. A really creepy doll. That's it. It's an old house, Faith. Abandoned for twenty-two months in foreclosure. Bound to find some weird things in here."

"I could do without finding creepy things. Weird, okay, but not creepy."

Don stole a glance at the girls. They were pulling every toy out from the box like it was Christmas. Seizing the opportunity of their distraction, he pinched Faith on the butt. She jumped and yelped, then slapped his hand away.

They ate dinner at their makeshift table. A kaleidoscope of boxes full of sesame chicken, sweet and sour chicken, and Mongolian beef stood posted around the table like warring tribes. After the girls picked at a few of the offerings and Don stuffed his face full, Faith whisked away the evidence of Don's caloric crime in a couple of minutes.

"I could get used to this, you know?" she said.

"Living out of boxes?"

"Not having any dishes, smart butt."

"Smart *butt!*" Brooke mimicked. Charity giggled and ran upstairs to put her pajamas on.

Don locked onto Brooke. Wrinkles formed around his eyes as he teased her. "You see that, dear?" he asked Faith. "How did we end up with only one responsible little girl?" Brooke stuck her tongue out at him and ran to catch up to Charity.

Once the girls were out of earshot, Faith whispered, "I've got something for you."

Don hesitated, having learned long ago not to misstep when presented with a moment like this. "I accept."

"You don't even know what it is!"

"You're right," he said slyly. "No idea. I'll just go straighten up our mattress on the floor."

"Don't go in there yet!"

Don kicked some of the boxes around for a few minutes, pretending to care about what was in what. He glanced back at the kitchen and caught her eye. "Okay, I'm ready." She smiled and took off for the bedroom. His first step slipped on the hardwood floor. When he caught up to her in the bedroom, he let out a sigh. The girls were sprawled diagonally on the mattress.

"Must have lost my mind thinking this would end any differently."

Faith smiled and rubbed the back of his neck. "We'll find time soon, I promise." She went to kiss him but a loud bang interrupted them. "What the hell was that?" she whispered.

He shook his head and started to the kitchen. She followed behind him as if they were attached. Scanning the main level, nothing was readily apparent. Suddenly, Faith pointed her finger at one of the three windows in the dining-room area. A bird hovered awkwardly on the ledge outside the window.

"Must've been that bird." They went over to the window. It was a medium-sized bird, nondescript and grayish-brown in color. When they were a few feet away, the bird took off into the tree just outside the house. "Strange."

Just as they started to turn back toward the bedroom, the bird banged into the window again. Faith shrieked and clenched onto Don's shoulders.

"What the hell . . ."

The bird hovered like it did before, took off from the window, and flew right back into it.

"Stop!"

Don struggled to figure out what he could do. The bird flew back and raced into the window again. This time, its neck snapped and it dropped like a stone out of view.

"Oh, my God!"

Don opened the back door and looked into the small garden outside the three windows. The bird was sprawled out on the ground. "Give me a plastic bag."

Faith handed him a bag from the Chinese restaurant. He averted his eyes while scooping up the bird and depositing it into a trash can. Faith shook her head when he walked back.

"What the heck was that?"

"Can't really explain it. Guess it was confused by the window."

He shut the door and gave Faith a quick hug. They returned to their room and squeezed in between the girls.

* * * * *

Leaves cluttered their side yard. Faith assigned them all chores for Saturday, and these damn leaves were his. He raked them into four piles and was bagging them when someone startled him from across the street. She was an older woman, slightly hunched over, maybe five-feet tall. Unkempt and frizzy hair sprouted from her scalp. A pair of faded purple sweats

12

covered her feeble legs. A white sweater with "Jamaica" spelled across the front of it engulfed the rest of her body.

Don stopped bagging and stood up. He waved and said hello, but a passing car drowned out both gestures. The wind blew and pushed parts of the last three piles across the lawn. Don cursed under his breath. When he went to grab the rake, he noticed that the woman was staring at him as if she hadn't seen him when she walked out of her own house. He waved again.

Her smile was almost imperceptible, and she reverted her focus to her own side yard. It consisted of a sidewalk and a narrow strip of flower bed that ran the entire block. It was very well kept, and included sunflowers and columbines and cherry blossom trees. Don bagged the last of the piles and moved the leaves behind the house for trash pickup. When he went back, the woman was staring at him again. He took this as an invitation to go over and talk.

Upon getting closer, he could discern the age in her face more accurately. Her movements were spry, but her face sagged and wrinkles interspersed her forehead and cheeks.

"You're the new neighbor," she said forcefully. Again, the strength of her voice didn't match the age of the mouth it escaped from.

"Yeah, my family too. We all moved in." He found himself strangely tongue-tied.

"Hopefully you take better care of that house than the last owner. He was a real strange one if you ask me." She spat out the word "strange," causing Don to straighten up slightly.

"Why's that?"

"Oh, just a weird one. Always having parties over there. Covering up the windows with bed sheets. You see it, don't you? He abused that house."

"Well, I can confirm he didn't take very good care of the house. I'm not sure how much of the condition was from the house being abandoned for so long versus from him, but there's plenty of neglect to go around."

"Bad shape?"

"Very."

"Our house wasn't in the best of shape when we bought it," she said, turning to the white mansion behind her. For this part of Denver, it was an enormous house. Faith told him on many occasions that the house was kind of like an unofficial landmark for people who had grown up in Denver. She loved digging into local history. It was white with an orange tile roof, Spanish villa style. Two chimney stacks jutted up past the peaks of the roof. Mature, evergreen landscaping wrapped around part of the house, shrouding the entries and backyard from peering eyes on the crisscrossing streets.

"Oh, yeah? Did you and your husband restore it?"

She scoffed at his comment. "My husband?" She left it there.

"Well, my name is Don, and it's really nice to meet you." He paused to consider his next move. "Maybe in a bit, after we've settled in, you can come over and we'll make you dinner. My wife is an excellent cook."

"I'd like that."

A car blasted its horn and distracted him from the conversation. When he turned to look back, the woman was already well down the sidewalk. He called out and asked what her name was, but another stiff wind snatched up his words.

T W O

THREE MONTHS LATER

Don perched over a workbench in the garage, trying to figure out how he was going to wire lights into the exposed ceiling of the garden-level room. He'd have to drill through the joists, so he grabbed a drill bit, but surmised it wouldn't be wide enough to fit the electrical cables. A cold wisp of air ran over his shoulders and down his back. The corner of the garage door never shut completely, allowing the wind in.

Then, something stomped in the room above the garage. He shook his head and slid the drill bit into the cordless drill. Crossing the door's threshold into the garden-level room, he screamed out for the girls to stop running around. No response. Don shook his head again and pulled his safety glasses down off the top of his head.

Just as his drill started, a beep sounded from their house alarm, signaling that a door had opened.

"Charity?" No response. "Brooke?!" He slid the glasses back onto his head and set the drill down. Concern rose in his chest. The front door led to two busy streets, neither of which he wanted the girls playing around. Starting toward the stairs, he yelled out again, "Charity!"

Don heard the sound of plastic bags. He got to the top of the steps just as Faith was walking in.

"What are you screaming about?"

"I was calling out for the girls. Where are they?"

"Down at the car, helping to get the groceries out."

"Wha—what do you mean?" She looked at him with exasperation. "I mean, were the girls with you?"

"Yeah, they went to the grocery store with me. What the heck's wrong, Don?"

"Were they inside the house?"

"Not yet—hey, what's wrong? You look pale."

After some consideration, he responded, "Nothing." Without another word, he returned to the garden level.

* * * * *

Don looked out from the French doors in their bedroom, watching the girls play with Philip in the backyard. The boy had been around to play with the girls on a few occasions. Oddly, he refused to come into the house, though, citing one excuse after another. Don tried to speak to the boy's parents about it, but they were always unavailable.

Philip stopped playing and looked directly up at Don. They stood there for several seconds, the girls running around Philip and prodding him to keep playing. The hair on the back of Don's neck rose, and he broke the stare when something thumped the ceiling above him.

"Faith?"

No answer. He left their bedroom, straining to hear that sound again. At the main level he called Faith's name out again, but still received no response. Leaning over the top of the steps to the garden level, he could hear the washing machine going and saw the faint glow of the laundry room light.

Girls were in back. Faith was in the laundry room. That sound had come from directly above him in the bedroom. He turned around and headed to the stairs to the top level. They were narrow, and had five steps up, a landing, and then five more steps up in the other direction. The attic was one area that Don had not been able to clean yet, and quite honestly, he hadn't spent any time up there. They also forbade the girls from being in the room, under the pretense that they could get hurt.

Don flicked a dirty switch and a dim light came on overhead. The glass dome for the fixture was almost blacked out with bugs. He looked more closely and saw they were miller moths. One fluttered in the pile and startled him. He laughed and glanced around.

Several boxes marked "U.S. Army" were strewn on the floor. Old newspaper bits announcing sales at Woolworth's covered most of the carpet. The attic was finished, albeit in a rather cheap fashion. At the top of the stairs there was a fifteen-foot-long by ten-foot-wide anteroom where all the mess resided. At the end of the space farthest from him there was a door. Thick wood, paint peeling. He remembered cracking the door open quickly to check inside when they were considering purchasing the house, but was surprised he hadn't investigated it much more.

Don slowly made his way to the door, taking in what he could in the low light. His palms became sweaty. He reached for the door and just as he did a small voice rose from behind him.

"Mr. Paxton."

Don's head just about hit the ceiling when he jumped and spun around. "Jesus!" He faintly felt a cold wisp of air glide over the beads of sweat that had collected on his forehead. "Philip! What the hell are you doing in here?"

Philip gestured toward the stairs and said, "Charity fell down and scraped her knee." Don watched the young boy's eyes and facial gestures. They were as placid and unaffected as a grazing cow. "She needs you," Philip added.

"Yeah," Don said. He headed down the steps to find Charity.

* * * * *

"When did you have time to do all this?" Don asked while looking over Faith's shoulder. She was sorting through a manila folder of pictures she had downloaded and printed out.

"Amazing, huh?"

"When were these photos taken?"

"Early nineteenth century." Don grabbed some of the photographs and methodically sorted through them. It was near impossible to identify the location in the pictures as Denver. The mountains were visible from the place where the picture was taken. Not a single tree, building or sign adulterated the view. This stood in stark contrast to what now existed when they looked out of their west-facing windows.

"Richthofen Castle," Faith said.

"Huh?"

"That's where the pictures were taken from. It explains why you can see all the way to the mountains. The castle is set above what we now know to be downtown Denver. It's a local treasure — the castle."

"Okay."

Faith snatched the photographs from him. "I thought you'd be a little more intrigued."

Don furrowed his eyebrows at her. "I was just taking my time to look. Where'd you get these? And, like I already asked, where'd you get time to research all this?"

"What do you care?"

"Well, 'cause I'm working my ass off, and you're off on some fishing expedition about local history."

Faith stopped rearranging the photographs and looked at him. "Say sorry."

"For what?" He looked at the ceiling and grimaced. "Sorry. Work is killing me right now."

"No reason to take it out on me." She stuffed them all back into the folder. The corner of one stuck out.

"What's that?"

She followed his finger back to the pile of photographs.

20

"Thought you didn't care."

"I *never* said that. Plus, that kind of looks like the corner of a . . ."

". . . casket. It is." She handed him that photograph. "It's a funeral. In a home."

"Why did you pull this one?" She let him analyze it longer. He started to shake his head. "No, no, no."

She nodded. "Afraid so."

"That's our living room."

"Sure is."

"Oh, man, how creepy."

"People die in homes all the time."

"Do they have the funeral *in the home* all the time?"

Faith took the photograph back from him and stood up. "That's not the worst part."

"The fact that an owner of this home died and had the funeral in that room right there isn't the worst part?"

"No, it's not." She took the folder and set it in an open drawer in the kitchen. She stirred the stew that she was making for dinner.

"Well, okay, master of suspense. I'm dying to hear the rest of the story now."

Faith faked like she was going to throw the spoon at him. "That's not an owner of the home."

Don paused, his face straining to understand what she was saying. "What's that?"

"The bottom of the photo. Go look at it."

He pulled the folder out from the drawer and sorted through it until he found the specific picture. "Wilma A. Russo."

"No Russo ever owned this home."

"Well, what if her husband owned it in his name? What if she was a family member of the owner?"

Faith smacked the wood ladle on the pot to knock the food off. "I did that digging. Wilma A. Russo, born February 23, 1860. Died December 2, 1916. Noted socialite in Denver. Married to Thomas B. Croke, who most certainly did not own this home."

"How do you know that?"

"Two reasons," she answered smugly. "First, I was able to pull the titled owners of this home from its inception. And, he wasn't on there. Second, Thomas B. Croke built the famed Croke-Patterson Mansion."

"So famed I haven't heard of it."

"And, you'll probably wish you never did."

"Hey, do you see this guy's figure is all blurred out in the picture?" Don asked, but any impending response was cut off by a cry.

"Dad!!"

Charity's voice yanked him from the conversation. There was a sense of urgency in her voice that only a parent could identify and distinguish from the myriad of other frantic calls he received from them. He rushed up the steps, following the sound of her second cry. She was in the finished attic, sitting in the corridor. One leg was tucked into her body. The other was stretched out. He could see a red mark on her shin, and a dainty stream of blood was trickling out of it onto the floor.

"What happened?" Charity just shook her head. "Honey, what happened?" Comforted by the tone of his voice, the tears started to well up in her eyes. He bent down and picked her up in his arms. He kissed her cheek and rubbed the back of her head. "Charity, what happened, honey? You're getting hurt left and right."

She looked him directly in the eyes, unwavering. Then, she turned around cautiously and pointed to the doll on the floor.

"The doll?" She nodded vigorously. "Oh, honey, I understand." He put his hand on the wrought iron railing and started down the steps. "You know, we all fall sometimes. It's really no big deal, honey. No need to blame it on the doll."

"But, Daddy, I didn't fall!"

He smiled. Charity always made up for her relative quietness with a huge imagination. "I thought I told you two to get rid of that doll, anyway."

"We did!"

He grinned again. "Okay, okay, I believe you. Well, let's get your leg bandaged up and then we'll figure out that doll, okay?"

She sunk her head into his shoulder. He reached the main level and gave Faith a thumbs up.

"She's okay?" He nodded. "How'd it happen?"

He considered how to respond. "The doll, the doll did it." They exchanged an understanding grin and he took Charity to clean her wound.

* * * * *

Rose sat stiffly in a chair in their living room. She had dressed up for the occasion, wearing a dark navy blue dress with gold stripes around the waist. She cleaned up so well that Don barely recognized her when she rang the doorbell.

Faith anxiously twirled her thumbs, a habit that ran back to her childhood. The girls sat equally as stiff as Rose. Don wondered how much longer they would last in this static state. Nine-year-old kids don't maintain decorum.

"Would you like one of these deviled eggs?"

"No, thank you, Faith. I've had plenty to eat today."

"I hope you saved some room for dinner."

"Oh, dear, I eat like a bird. Just peck here and there. I'd much rather we were able to sit by this fire and just chat a little."

Don toyed with his winter beard. Right as he was throwing clothes on, he caught a glimpse of himself in the mirror. Sunken eyes, black half-moons under them. A pale, sickly pallor. Bloodshot eyes. He had just wrapped up two months of preparing for two trials that didn't end up going forward. That meant he finished this last week with the flu and vapors in his gas tank. With all the work, he had completely forgotten about inviting Rose over for dinner until Faith reminded him this morning. Now, though, he wondered if it was such a good idea.

"Rose, why don't I show you around the house?"

"Kind of you, Donald, but I've been in here before."

"You have?" Faith asked.

Brooke tugged at the sleeve of Don's blazer. All of their formal wear made him question whether they hadn't brought this on themselves. Dressing this way didn't leave room for anything other than stuffiness. He nodded to Brooke and she took off to the garden level to watch television. Charity stayed, silent and meek as a mouse on one of the plush, chocolate brown leather chairs surrounding the fireplace.

"Yes, yes. My husband and I have lived in our house for over forty years. We've known many of the occupants of this house. Your house."

Don and Faith exchanged a look, not sure if they wanted to know any more about the house than they did. Ignorance truly was bliss, and Faith had already jeopardized that with her digging. The wood in the fireplace crackled and sent embers up the flue. Don made out the faintest hint of the honey-baked ham Faith had in the oven. He looked back at the chair where Charity had been, and she was gone.

"Well, what can you tell us about the previous owners?"

Rose smiled and crossed her legs, then set her hands gently on her knees. "There have been quite a few in the past five years. The last was a businessman who moved in with his fiancée. He was the chief executive of a local bank. They were engaged for just nine months."

"From the tone of your voice, it doesn't sound like it ended all that well," Don said.

"He came home one day to find her in that level," she said, pointing to the garden level, "with another man."

"Oh, goodness," Faith murmured.

"And, a woman."

Don's eyebrows shot up. "Holy cow!"

"Yes, holy cow. Naturally, they were through after that. J.R. — that was his name — continued to live there for a little over a year longer. We saw very little of him. That's when the house truly started to deteriorate."

"It wasn't always like this?" Faith asked.

"No, heavens no! This house used to rival ours. A magnificent landscape in the front. Mrs. Sturling would take the time to plant annuals every year. They had a beautiful weeping willow that I watched grow for fifteen years. When that tree died, so did the house."

"Who were the Sturlings?"

Rose smiled. She had a bottom row of crooked teeth that were only visible when she smiled. "Mr. Benjamin Sturling was a local lawyer. A plaintiff's lawyer, if I recall correctly. He was quite a character. Lively, loved his cars. He had the first Porsche I had ever seen in person. He even let me drive it," she said with reminiscent warmth. The oven beeped.

"Oh, hold on! I've got to go check the ham," Faith said.

Don let out a long sigh. As he drew in, he could smell the ham, but also picked up on something else. Before he could place it, Rose said, "I haven't seen you outside that much, Donald."

"I know. I've just been too busy. Feels like I've been shuttling myself to work in the dark, and doing the same on the way back. I haven't had a breath of natural air in several weeks."

"That's a real shame. Being cooped up at this time of year is not good for anyone."

"You're telling me," Faith added, returning from the kitchen. "I'm not sure a person can ever get used to the days getting dark by five."

"The weather has been no excuse to stay inside, though," Rose said. "I will tell you, my weary old bones do *not* mind this warm weather at all."

A plate clinked in the kitchen, and the next thing Don saw was Charity coming with something in her hands.

"Mrs. White, I made some cookies for you."

Don smiled, never tiring of Charity's kindness. He looked up at Rose's face and was surprised to see her looking perplexed.

"Rose?"

She glanced up at him. Then, she stroked Charity's long, brown ponytail. "This was so kind. You are a darling." She daintily took one of the cookies. "There aren't many children like you left in this world, it seems to me."

Charity's cheeks turned red, and she offered the plate to Don, who gladly took a cookie too. "Nothing like dessert first." Don took two bites of his cookie before Rose had even taken a bite herself. "I'm sorry, I'm a darn glutton."

"No worries, Donald. Like I said before, I eat like a bird." She took a nibble of the cookie and her eyes lit up. "Delicious, Charity! Just delicious."

The attention was enough to drive Charity from the room in a fit of joy and embarrassment.

"Where were we?" Rose asked. "I'm afraid that cookie completely distracted me!"

"I think you were telling us about the Sturlings?"

"Ah, yes. Mr. Sturling, a real gentleman. Mrs. Sturling was equally as energetic as her husband. She spent so much time

28

outside in her gardens. Both the front and the back. As the saying goes, her thumbs were truly green."

"I can't say the same for myself," Faith bemoaned.

"It can be acquired, my dear." She stopped and mulled over her next words. "It can also be lost. I have spent much time looking across at this house watching the gardens die. They withered away just like the occupants of the house."

"What do you mean?" Don asked.

Rose dabbed at her eye with a piece of tissue she had tucked in between her wrist and sweater. Recounting the story finally got the best of her. With a shake of her head she said, "The day they found all of them. The whole family, dead for all intents and purposes. The sound of the sirens still haunts my waking eyes. And, that poor child of theirs. To have him die so young is just not right."

"Oh, no," Faith gasped.

Rose took a deep breath in through her nose. "I'm so sorry. It was just such a tragedy. I still remember the day they found him."

"How old was he?" Don asked.

"Just nine. He was an odd boy. Rather quiet in contrast to his parents. He spent a fair amount of time with me. I believe us introverts tend to be magnetized to one another," she said, her eyes welling over with tears again.

"What was his name?"

"Oh, Don, stop the lawyering. Can't you see how this affects Rose?" Faith ran to a bathroom on the bedroom level to grab more tissues. She got back and handed them to Rose.

"Thank you, Faith." Rose dabbed her eyes and then her nose. "His name was Philip."

THREE

1961

Philip ignored his mother's calls to come to dinner. He stared out of the side window on the main level, his hands steady on the red tile windowsill. The cold wind of late fall blustered by the house, and he could feel its power even through the window.

He watched Mrs. White tend to her garden across the street, then heard his mom's footsteps stomping his way. Irritation was evident in every pound on the floor. Mrs. White met his eyes for a flash of time before he was lifted into the air.

"I called you, Philip Charles. I called you several times, and I told you how your dad gets when he's hungry." She carried him by his underarms to the dining room table. His dad was sitting there, eyes red and slightly glazed. A stabbed piece of pork chop moved into his mouth. Philip chewed robotically before spitting the piece back onto the plate. Both of his parents stopped.

His dad smiled. Nothing warm about it. He wasn't sure if he'd ever seen his dad smile warmly. No, this smile meant something altogether different.

"Don't want to eat that food, do you?" Philip shook his head no. His dad shrugged his shoulders. "I don't blame you. This food is *shit*!" he said as he slammed his plate on the table. Philip's mom buried her head in her hands.

"You don't want to eat, huh?" This time, Philip didn't respond. "Come on, boy! You were so averse to eating your food just a few seconds ago. You didn't change that quickly, did you?"

His dad leaned over the table, getting close to his face. Philip could smell the alcohol. He knew what it meant at this point. Veins bulged in his dad's neck and eyes. Those dark, hollowed-out cavities around his eyes. Red skin, always red.

"What do you think we should do with her?"

"Daddy, no. I'll eat it now!"

"Listen to you, coming to her aid." His dad picked up the morning's newspaper and rapped it on his hand. "You can defend your mom, but you can't do something as simple as eat her terrible food. I just don't get it." One of his dad's hands grabbed his mom's shoulder.

"Missie, let's go to the room."

Philip's mom started sobbing. He felt a lump in his throat. He wanted to throw up, or cry, or run around the table and pound his hands on his dad's legs.

"Benjamin, please don't do this again. Please, my dear."

His dad stopped and smiled that unforgiving smile. "My dear, if you'd made a damn child that listened, we wouldn't have this problem."

Next thing Philip knew, he was trailing both of his parents up the flight of steps to the bedroom level. He never understood how his mom, so much taller and bigger than his dad, failed to fight back. Philip just hung onto her dress, trying to use his slight weight to stop their momentum.

"You want to come too, that why you're holding on?" Philip

looked into his dad's eyes as his father took a break in the hallway between the two bedrooms. Then, he dragged Philip's mom up the final flight of stairs to the attic.

"Philip, leave us alone. Go play in your bedroom, honey." Philip didn't let go of the dress. He couldn't let go of his mom. "Philip! Go away!" His small hands loosened and his mom's dress flew out of them. She watched him lifelessly as she allowed herself to be pulled up the steps. Philip's lip shuddered when she was lifted out of sight, having reached the top of the steps in the attic. He heard the door to the room slam shut, and then he heard his mom's familiar sounds.

* * * * *

"Philip! Philllipppp!" He faintly registered the voice in his mind. Something tugged at his elbow. Sounds of kids playing on the playground resurfaced to his conscious awareness. The brisk winter air pricked his cheeks. It was Chelsea, just about the only person in his class who paid him any mind. She craned her neck to see over his shoulder, and saw a worm cut up in segments in front of him.

"Philip, what are you doing?" she asked with an exaggerated look of frustration on her face. "Why don't you come play with the rest of us?" He only shook his head. "Well, walk home together like usual?"

He'd likely never admit it to anyone, but he never wanted to miss one of those walks home with her. It was the only gentle, peaceful time in his life. The only time when he could let his guard down. He nodded. Chelsea smiled and sprinted back to the game of dodgeball going on in the yard.

The rest of the day moved by as slowly as a fifty-car train. Ms. Lint tottered on in front of them. Philip tried to stave away the daydreams filled with replays of the events of the night before. Slowly and methodically, he traced a circle on his paper.

"Mr. Sturling. *Mr. Sturling.* Are you listening to me?" Philip looked up and the rest of the class was staring at him. He could see the disdain in their eyes. Their collective belief that something was wrong with him. Like when the herd identifies a sick member and does everything it can to avoid it.

He heard himself say, "Yes, Ms. Lint." He stared through her until she glanced away uncomfortably. Then, he went back to tracing his circle. The school bell rang mercifully and all of the children scrambled for the classroom door, except for Philip. He folded his paper in half, and then in half again. He looked up and saw Chelsea patiently waiting for him.

"Mr. Sturling, would you please exit the classroom like the rest of your colleagues?" Ms. Lint fixed her good eye on him. "You know, it's rather strange that you would turn out so melancholy with the upstanding parents you have, Mr. Sturling. Perhaps, you should take a lesson from your father in how to treat other people like a gentleman." He packed the remainder of his materials—two pencils and a pink rubber eraser—into his sack. Chelsea put her arm around his shoulder when he got to the door.

"The long way home?" He assented.

The long way was about a half a mile longer, through parts of Crestmoor and Montclair. They ran over Monaco Parkway and headed up the hill. Branches of dead trees towered over them and creaked in the abnormally strong wind. Chelsea buttoned up her blue uniform jacket and Philip slipped his cotton gloves on.

They walked in silence for half the trip. Chelsea never could contain herself though, and she started up on school, friends, and her family's upcoming trip to California in December.

"What about you, Philip? Are you and your family going to stay here for Christmas?"

"We never travel. Father doesn't like it."

"Why not?"

"He doesn't like driving long distances." Philip kicked a pile of leaves left by a homeowner. "And, mom doesn't drive."

"You have heard of airplanes, right?"

"Too much money."

"Philip! Your family has money. You're rich!"

He shot her a look that temporarily suspended her good-natured ribbing. "Father says we have money because we don't spend it."

"You know, that old toad Ms. Lint is right about one thing, Philip. You're too down. What's wrong?"

He ignored the question and they returned to silent walking. They reached the castle and Philip stopped.

"Philip," Chelsea whispered, "Let's not stop here." She grabbed his hand and tried to pull him, but he was cemented in place. "Come *onnnnn*, this place is so creepy."

Philip's face was expressionless. He studied the elaborate parapets on the castle.

"Fine, I'm leaving then," Chelsea said with her hands on her hips. Philip went up to the double swing gate flanked by stone masonry walls. Crispy paint flaked off the gate when he touched it. The metal seemed colder than it could have or should have been. A crow barked out at him from one of the trees that obscured the castle from view with their leaves during the spring and summer months. Now the dark limbs of the trees just reached out to a big, blue nothing of a sky that yielded only frigid air.

He moved to his right, keeping his left hand on the gate and letting it hit every welded baluster. The rosettes decorating the ends of the gate clung on while he did this, adding to the rattle. Philip stopped and looked down the hill toward his home, and toward Chelsea's. She was now several blocks away. He traced his steps back along the gate, repeating the prior process.

Something rustled the dead leaves on the ground. Philip froze mid-step and tried to place the sound with something around him. Then, he saw it. A squirrel foraged through the leaves, looking for an acorn buried in warmer times. He heard a puff and the squirrel chirped angrily while jumping to the side. Another puff and the squirrel fell on its side, jolting its legs as if it had lost all control of them. It stopped moving just as the man came up to the gate.

"What are you doing here, Philip?" Philip's little hand was clenched around one of the tubes of the gate. The man pried it off. He was tall, very slender, almost too slender to survive in the

36

bitter cold visiting them this winter. A wisp of hair stuck out from the front of a flannel cap with fur-covered ear warmers. Philip couldn't tell if this man was really old or not. He couldn't tell if this man was threatening or not. He just froze.

"How — how do you know my name?"

The man studied him. "It's dangerous to play around this castle."

"Why?" All sights, sounds, and smells separate from the man had vanished. The entirety of Philip's attention was focused on him.

The man raised an eyebrow. "You know why."

"Evil."

The man nodded. Philip stuck his hands in his pockets and walked away from the gate, checking back over his shoulder on two occasions. There was no further sign of the man.

* * * * *

Philip sat alone on one of the red school benches eating his lunch. A peanut butter and jelly sandwich, stick of cheese and apple were neatly arranged in front of him on his brown paper bag. He sipped on a juice and heard their footsteps before their voices.

"Phil, Phil the pill. Always alone, ain't ya?" Philip didn't look up, didn't move. That was the voice of Patrick O'Brien, a boy of medium height, with disheveled brown hair and freckles on his face. He slammed his fist down on Philip's sandwich, sending jelly squirting onto the tabletop of the bench. Philip blinked his eyes several times.

Someone smacked him on the back of the head. "Where's your girlfriend?" Brian Flynn mocked him. "Chelseeeea. Chelsea, where are you!?"

"Oh man, you're *such* a baby, Philip. Don't you ever wonder why people don't like you?"

"Blockhead."

Philip grabbed his brown bag and tried to start putting his lunch away. Patrick snatched the bag from his hands and ripped it in two.

"You don't need that." Philip tried to put the apple in his pocket. Brian hit the apple with his hand. Philip cried out.

"Cut it out!"

"Cut it out! Cut it out!" Both of the boys mimicked him.

Philip looked around desperately, but there were no teachers in sight.

Patrick laughed. "There's no one here to help you, Phil the pill." He grabbed Philip's white collared shirt and twisted it until Philip shrieked. "You're coming with us."

The boys dragged him to the nearby girl's bathroom.

"This is where you belong, ain't it?" Brian said. "In here with the *girrrrls*." Philip shook his head. "Yes, you do! Look, you've even got one of these on you," Brian added as he threw something into Philip's lap.

"What—what is that?" It was white, cylindrical and had a string hanging out of the back of it. Both of the boys giggled.

"What is it? That's just something we found out on the playground. Must be someone's toy." Philip looked at the thing skeptically. "Now listen, Phil." Philip looked up. "If you leave this bathroom, I'm gonna kick the shit out of you. Got me?"

"I'm not staying in the girl's bathroom. I'll get in trouble!"

Patrick came over and hit him on the ear. "No shit, you little dweeb. That's the point." Philip rubbed his ear. He could feel his teeth grinding. "You see how that one hit feels? It'll be a whole lot more if you leave this bathroom before I tell you to. Got it?" Patrick kicked one of Philip's legs and walked out of the bathroom.

Philip sat on the floor where he had fallen back under the pressure of both boys. He started to cry but then heard his dad's voice in his head. "Don't be a goddamn baby, Philip!" He wiped his eyes and went to get up.

Right then, he heard a chorus of girls' voices. The door opened before he could try to find a spot to hide, let alone brace for their reactions. Their screams rattled around the small, completely tiled bathroom. Philip froze, the tampon in his hand, the girls wide-eyed and screaming in unison until their little voices gave out. Two teachers responded to the alarm, pushed the girls aside and stopped when they saw Philip cowering in the back of the bathroom. His shirt was crumpled around his neck. His hair was matted to one side. A shoelace was undone. What he had in his hand surprised them most. This time, no voice in his head could stop the flow of tears.

*****

Philip sat across from his dad at the dinner table. This was essentially the only place they ever saw each other. When home, his dad spent most of his time in the attic room, drinking, working, staring at walls, whatever. Mom set a plate of food down in front of his dad. They all shared a common tension. Dinner was always as unpredictable as two dice bouncing around a craps table. His dad dug into the first bite and didn't say anything. Another bite. This time his dad smiled.

"Very good, Missie. Hot and ready for me. You've even got a piece of bread here. See, it isn't that hard to make a man happy."

His mom let out a relieved puff of air and smiled back. Then she went back into the kitchen and prepared Philip's plate.

"How was school today, Philip?" The question immediately drew Philip back to the day at school. To the time in the principal's office with Mrs. Thompson, a short, blond-haired lady who frightened the hell out of him. Going into her office was like walking through the gates of Oz and seeing the wizard. His dad's jaw stopped chewing.

"Philip, I asked you a question."

"Sir?"

"How was school? You got a damn hearing problem now?"

Philip shook his head. "It was fine, thank you."

40

His dad took another bite, then set down his fork. That confused Philip. His dad never stopped eating before his plate was absolutely cleaned off, or before he pushed it away in disgust. His mom stopped what she was doing. Their old stove made the only sound, blowing flames to keep the remaining food warm.

"That's not what I heard."

"Sir?"

"I said, that's not what I heard." Philip looked at his mom, confused. He could see the terror start to work its way onto her face.

"Mrs. Thompson called me, at work. Said that you were found in the girl's bathroom—"

"I was forced in there!"

His dad slammed his hands on the table. "Don't you interrupt me! You know I hate that!" His mom started to move toward them. "Stay where you are, Missie. This is a thing between us men."

"He's not a man, Benjamin."

"I'm thinking you're right after hearing this goddamn story. Found your little fancy boy in the girl's bathroom, holding a tampon. A *goddamn* tampon, Missie! You letting him get into your stuff?"

His mom swept over to them, placing herself behind Philip.

41

"I'm sure there is some explanation, right, honey?" Philip nodded his head.

"Explanation or not, you lied to me, didn't you, Philip? Your day wasn't fine, was it?"

"I didn't want to bother you with it, Daddy."

"For Christ's sake, stop calling me Daddy."

"Please don't take the Lord's name in vain, not in front of Philip," Missie said.

His dad stood up from his chair. "Well, shit, Missie. Is that better?" He pointed at Philip. "Get up, you're coming with me."

"No, Benjamin, please let him explain."

"Don't you get it, Missie? I don't care about the explanation. I care about the lie!"

"He was scared, he was just scared, Benjamin."

"I don't care." His dad grunted as he grabbed a hold of Philip's arm and yanked him out of the chair.

"No, Benjamin, please no!" She grabbed onto his shoulder but he shook her off. "Take me. Just take me, please!"

His dad stopped near the first flight of stairs up to the bedroom level. He looked down at Philip. "Well, sissy boy, it'll be your decision." He grinned. "You want your mommy to take your place?

Philip slumped to his knees. He looked at his mom.

"Yes, yes, Philip." She held her hands out to him. Her lower lip quivered. "Come to Momma."

Teary eyes looked back up at his dad. The man appeared to be carved from stone, ready to move upon the whisper of an answer. The V formed between his eyebrows didn't relent. His grin stayed perfectly immobile. Philip shook his head no.

"Philip! Oh, Philip!" his mom wailed. His dad dragged him up to the room.

The room was in the attic, at the end of a short hallway. The hallway, the anteroom, and the rest of their house were immaculately kept. The room was a different story, largely because Philip's mother was not allowed in under any circumstances. Unless Dad forced her in.

Philip had only been in the room one time before and so didn't recall it well. In fact, it was almost like he was entering the room for the first time. The wallpaper was peeling off. The room seemed damp, from what source it was impossible to tell. A tall window at the other end of the room, stretching from the floor to the ceiling, was barred off. A bed sheet hung over the window to keep away the prying eyes. To maintain the fallacy that the Sturlings were a hardworking, upper-middle-class family with their act together.

Philip tried to sputter out some words, but couldn't muster all of the energy necessary.

The floor outside of the room was carpeted. Inside it was just hardwood. The finish was worn away in most places. All sorts of scrapes and scratches crisscrossed the floor like lashes on skin.

His father let him drop to the ground and went over to a candle. He snapped a match off on the side of the box and lit that candle, then two others. The rest of the furnishings of the room came into being, illuminated by the flighty candle flames. A plush, brown leather chair grew out of one corner. The leather on the arms was rubbed down to a different color. The front of the chair looked like it had liquid spilled on it. Philip was on his side right next to a table that ran the entire length of the room. Several shiny, metal objects hung from small hooks on the side of the table. There was an overhead light, but it was blacked out.

"I've only given you a few rules," his father said while falling back into the chair. His dad instantly started to rub the arms of the chair with his hands. "What's number one?"

"No lying."

"No lying—what?"

"No lying, sir."

"That's right. No lying. You violated that rule, agreed?" Philip nodded. "You would agree that you should be punished for that, right?"

"Yes, sir."

His dad didn't say anything else, and his eyes slowly closed. Philip thought he heard his mom outside of the room. His dad's eyes remained shut, his hands rested on the chair like two overworked giants. The silence was long enough that Philip thought his dad may have fallen asleep. Somehow, by some act of grace. A fast move to the door could get him out. He knew he could make it before his dad did.

But, what then?

There was no escaping this. He couldn't run into the street and get help. He couldn't just run away. Then, the energy that charged his mind changed polarities as he set his eyes on the gleaming, stainless steel tools hanging from the table. He couldn't run, but maybe he could fight.

Just as one of his little, pale hands was about to grab the wood handle of a curved blade, his father's eyes snapped open.

"Those are Daddy's tools." There was no blinking, no facial expression, but his father's eyes communicated everything necessary. Philip sat back on his butt. His dad stood up from the chair. It almost looked like he levitated. He grabbed Philip by the back of his neck with one rough hand.

"I've consulted myself, and I'm prepared to issue your punishment. Drop your pants."

This time, Philip was certain the sound he heard outside of the room was his mom. A shriek, then begging and pleading. Philip dropped his pants as instructed. His dad snatched a bottle off of a side table next to the chair and removed the stop. He looked at Philip and then took a long swig. He came over next to Philip, who had assumed the position to get spanked on the table.

Philip could feel his dad's warm breath, could smell the liquid he had just drunk. "I need you to stop being such a baby, you got me?" His dad slammed the glass bottle down on the table next to Philip's head. "Next time those kids hassle you," his dad put a closed fist in front of his face, "do something bad to them."

There were several seconds of breathing. Philip's legs started shaking. He sunk his head down on the table. Then, he heard the door to the room open and his dad said, "Get out of the fucking way" to his mom. Philip lifted his head and looked around. It was just him in the room. His mom was on her hip, leaning on one of her hands. The other hand wiped the streams of tears from her cheeks.

Philip lifted his pants up and buttoned them, then zipped the zipper. He moved out of the room and closed the door. His mom's blood-red eyes watched him. She reached out and he avoided her touch, then headed down the stairs.

F O U R

There were plenty of days where Philip daydreamed of having superpowers. Being invincible so he could hammer Patrick and Brian's faces in. Flying so he could get away from them while bellowing. Invisibility so he could embarrass them in a classroom or out at lunch. He rode his bike down a winding street, thinking about what he would do to them. What he was going to do to them.

He passed the low chain-link fence that surrounded the polo grounds and then the high school he was supposed to transition to after he finished middle school. Pine trees stood out with their bushy foliage next to the skeletons of other trees. He looked both ways at a stop sign and went through it with the slightest pause. The dirt road up to his school loomed ahead with its big hill. He gathered speed, stood up out of the saddle, and powered up the incline.

He felt like he could lift a ship with one hand.

The bell rang seconds after he locked his bike up to a rack. He hustled to his classroom, greeted by the glower of Ms. Lint. A piece of wadded-up paper flew across the classroom and hit him on the cheek.

"Okay, now who did that?!"

All of the students looked down, except for Philip and except for Patrick. They stared at each other while the rest of the students giggled into their chests. Ms. Lint, as ineffective as ever, huffed and puffed a few more times and then told Philip to pick up the paper.

"Now go sit down, Mr. Sturling," she said with tight hands on her hips.

"Ms. Lint?"

Her eyebrows dropped. Her jaw tightened. "Yes, Mr. Sturling?"

"May I please sharpen my pencil?"

She nodded. Philip stuck a number two pencil into the sharpener and spun the handle. He felt the rotary blade turn and grind away the dull tip. Staring through the classroom windows, he felt the cold air come in and immediately get confronted by the excess heat from the old boiler. After the grinding stopped, Philip headed back to his chair and turned to a new page in his notebook. He listened to Ms. Lint to make sure he wouldn't be caught off guard with any questioning. Time crawled by until the bell finally rung for recess. Philip meticulously put his notebook and erasers into his backpack. A slot on the outside of his backpack housed the freshly sharpened pencil. Ms. Lint watched him leave the classroom and she shut the door behind him with her glare still tattooed on his neck.

The schoolyard was enormous. It had a grass field the size of a city block. A playground loomed on one side. He typically avoided playing in it because there were too many places where Brian or Patrick could beat him up out of sight. A large parking lot with several basketball hoops framed the other side of the schoolyard. In front of the field was a twenty-foot-high handball wall. Philip generally took to playing by himself behind a row of hedges at the far end of the field. There were about ten feet between the hedges and a wood fence protecting homes on the other side.

He made his way along his normal route. Every step on this route was planned to avoid running into Patrick or Brian. Through the outside lunch benches. Behind the handball wall to the playground, where a huge oak tree provided shadows. Then, to the hedges. The intent behind the route was always there, but the results were almost always similar.

"Hey, Phil the Pill, come back here to your little dollhouse?"

He kept walking down the length of hedges. The footsteps behind him were constant, even, and made by more than one person.

"Blockhead, I'm talking to you! Don't make me chase you down."

Philip looked through one of the breaks in the hedges and saw Mr. Garrett, the ancient man who supervised the yard during recesses. He was close to the parking lot side of the field, a healthy distance from where they were. Philip kept walking.

"Brian, you catch this? The Pill ain't gonna stop for us today. Forget it, I could use a run."

Philip took off first, knowing that the stronger boys would catch up to him quickly. He grabbed the pencil from the side of the backpack now swinging chaotically. Someone stumbled behind him and hit the ground with a thud. Brian cried out, loud enough for Mr. Garrett to hear. Philip felt the pound of Patrick's feet close behind him. He imagined Patrick's thin, blond hair rocking back and forth with each stride. He waited until he felt the hand grab his backpack, and then he swung his right hand

49

around.

The pencil stabbed directly into Patrick's left eye. Philip stood there, panting as Patrick went into shock. One of his hands shot up and swiped at the pencil, but the glancing blow only twisted it sideways. That's when he screamed. So loud, so crazed. Nothing Philip had ever heard before.

Philip started screaming too and fell to the ground. He scraped his face on the ground and clawed the ground with his fingers. He bit his tongue as hard as he could and yelped. Tears flowed out of his eyes. Next thing he knew, he was suspended in the air. Through blurry vision, he saw Mr. Duggan, the vice principal. As Mr. Duggan hauled him away from the hedges, he continued crying, but just quietly enough to be able to hear Patrick.

* * * * *

Mrs. Thompson sat behind her desk, like an enthroned statute that blinked sporadically. Light blush augmented her pale skin. A half-dome of blue eye shadow cradled her brown eyes. The walls of her office were covered with framed photographs and awards. Not that it mattered to Philip, but he had heard some of the comments of parents and teachers that Mrs. Thompson was a highly respected principal.

She had the pencil on her desk and rolled it over to him.

"This was in Mr. O'Brien's eye, as I'm sure you're aware." She studied him, watching for any reaction. Philip remained stoic. "And, I'm sure your story is that this pencil ended up in Mr. O'Brien's eye by some random accident, correct?"

50

"They were chasing me."

"That doesn't answer my question."

"They were chasing me and they fell on me. Well, Patrick did."

"These two have bullied you for quite some time, right? We've had talks about your interactions with them." Philip didn't see a need to respond verbally. Mrs. Thompson pulled the pencil back and put it into a paper bag.

"How are things at home?"

"Fine." He could smell her heavy perfume. He analyzed her perfectly cut, blond bob-cut hair. She was just over five feet tall. Those feet must not touch the ground when she sits in her chair, he thought.

"When I tell your dad about this, how do you think he will respond?"

"Like he always does."

Mrs. Thompson's eyes narrowed. "How is that?"

"Angry. Yelling. He will probably hit me or my mom."

Mrs. Thompson let out a blip of a laugh. "Your faculty with deception is astounding. Coming from a nice family like yours, I am surprised you would act this way. Some people mistake your quiet nature for a shy child. I never bought that, for even a moment. I know how you really are." She pursed her lips and let the silence ripen between them again.

"I'm obviously not in a position to reprimand you regarding this incident, yet. You know that, don't you?" Without waiting for his response, she continued, "I will inform your father of what happened today. I will also inform him of the disparaging comments you made regarding him."

That comment elicited the only detectable reaction from Philip. His hands jerked together in a small movement, then they reset in his lap.

"Most people spend their lives hacking at the branches on the tree of evil, Philip. Most can never identify just where to strike. I can recognize the root of it. I recognize it in you. I will find a way to link intention to this incident, and you will be gone from here forever." He looked up from his lap with just his eyes. "You may be excused."

He picked up his backpack and left Mrs. Thompson's office.

* * * * *

After the talk with Mrs. Thompson, he was excused from the last hour of the day. When the office threatened to call his parents to pick him up, he begged and pleaded to just ride his bike home. They finally acquiesced and he unlocked his bike and then walked down the steep dirt hill away from the school. The ruts in the hill had sent him tumbling one too many times for him to chance riding it. Deep in thought, deep in reflection of the incident, he didn't notice Chelsea's ponytail flick out from behind a tree at the bottom of the hill. She hopped out onto the road when he got there. It startled him enough that he dropped the bicycle, grabbed both straps of his backpack, and just stood there.

"I thought you were Brian."

"That's the meanest thing you've ever said to me." Chelsea picked up the bicycle and started to walk away from him. He followed. As per usual, they didn't say anything for a few blocks. The sound of his front wheel clicking set their pace.

Chelsea broke the silence. "I heard what happened."

"How did you get out of class?"

"I went to the bathroom and never went back."

"Really?"

"Yep."

"They're going to be looking for you."

"I know."

He couldn't believe she'd done this, but said nothing more about it.

"Was it an accident?" she asked.

"Of course."

They walked down the winding street that Philip loved to cruise on. Right at this location, the trees and bushes on either side of the road closed in to form a living tunnel. Chelsea stopped.

"I didn't just skip out on class and put my butt on the line with my parents to get a lie from you." Her delicate facial features managed to look hard at him. "Don't lie to me."

Philip didn't know how to respond. She had never been tough with him. She had never demanded anything in their friendship. Yet, there she stood, all four feet of her, in her navy blue, plaid school skirt and black shoes with socks up to her ankles. The ponytail wasn't bouncing exuberantly now. It, too, had assumed the serious tone of its wearer.

"It wasn't an accident," Philip whispered.

Her eyebrows didn't raise up. Her body didn't pull back. There were no signs that had expected any other answer. She pivoted around and kept walking.

Without turning around, she said, "I knew you would do it someday." No more words were spoken until they reached the point where the trip could be extended by going to the castle. Philip stopped.

"What's the problem?"

"I'm going up there."

That was enough of a description for Chelsea to know what he was talking about. She handed him his bike.

"I believed I saw something good in you, Philip. I guess I was wrong." He was confused. Tears formed in her eyes, but she walked away before they could escape.

He got on his bike and rode up the hill to the castle. A car crept past him containing an old man who stared at him with eyes white as a polished stone. Philip studied the car as it pulled into the castle's rear entrance. A man got out and then leaned on the gate to close it. Philip recognized him as the man he had talked to before.

He rode slowly, pushing down hard on each pedal stroke, his eyes fixated in front of him. Once he rounded a corner of the castle, he stopped and pushed his bike under some unkempt bushes. Minutes passed as he waited there, crouched against the stone fence. After he had seen no indication of movement for a while, he went back toward the gate. Reaching one side of it, he peeked around a column to see if anyone was there. The coast was clear. The gate was huge and made of thick wrought iron. Philip yanked on the latch that affixed the gate into the ground and pushed with all his weight. It moved just enough for him to slip his body through.

Gravel crunched under his feet. Things seemed subtly different within the gates. Sounds were magnified. The wind blew harder. The air was colder. His senses were on overdrive. The driveway never seemed to end. He just kept walking until by some miracle he reached the back side of the castle. This part of the castle was never visible from the street. It raised the hairs on the back of his neck to be treading in uncharted territory. Philip stopped in an archway with steps leading up to a door. All of a sudden, a voice rasped from behind him.

"We get kids like you every few years or so." Philip spun around to see the man with the white eyes. A cane jutted up from under the man's overcoat. "Too damn curious for their own good."

"Who—who are you?"

"Never mind that. This is my property, I will ask the questions. Who are *you*? And, I want your last name to be able to call your wretched parents."

Philip was stunned. The possibility of getting caught was never far from his mind. However, face-to-face with this bent-over man, actually caught now, threw him. The man whacked his cane against the side of the castle.

"I asked you, child, what is your full name?"

"Philip Sturling."

"Well, Philip Sturling, get in that door and sit down while I ring your parents." The door opened and Philip saw the man from before. He considered running past the blind man, but that cane was swinging back and forth like a divining rod. Plus, the opportunity to see the inside of the castle outweighed the whipping he was sure to get from his parents. At least, it did in the short term.

Inside, the castle was bitterly cold. A fire crackled somewhere in the distance. The blind man shut the door himself.

"Bradley, ring Mr. and Mrs. Sturling to let them know their little son has trespassed on my property."

Philip wondered how the man could know anything about him, particularly anything regarding how he appeared. The castle was extremely dark inside. Little light penetrated the heavy curtains drawn on every window. To Philip's left was a study, lined with books from floor to ceiling. Candles lit the room. The blind man guided Philip to a chair with his cane.

56

"Wow," Philip said as he passed a full-size replica of a knight in armor. The cane smacked his hand just as he was about to touch it. "Ouch!"

"No one invited you here to touch things."

The blind man made his way over to a desk and chair with surprising deftness. Philip sat in his appointed chair and air escaped from the leather cushion. Something smelled. It was unfamiliar to him.

"Don't try to sneak out of that chair, young man. I have uncanny senses." The blind man rested his cane against the giant desk, leaned back and sighed.

Philip studied the books on the shelves. A beat-up ladder stood in front of them. The vague outline of daylight shown through the curtains. A skinned bear lay on the floor in between them, its agape mouth revealing monstrous teeth.

"So, who are you?"

"Do you frequently break into someone's home and then ask *them* who they are?" The blind man lowered his head when he spoke, and raised it back up to meet any response.

"I've never done this before."

"Well, I'm privileged to have been the first."

Philip couldn't rest without knowing who this man was. His restlessness must have been tangible enough for his opposing party to feel.

"How old are you?" he asked the man.

"You're quite brazen for someone who can't be a day over nine years old. I am Walter von Richthofen, the second."

Philip hesitated. "Are you . . . royalty?"

The man snorted. "No, just German."

The other man came back into the room. "I was able to connect with the boy's father at his place of employment."

Walter nodded. Philip's heart jumped into his throat. His father having to leave work? Again, the old man sensed something.

"What's wrong, child? *Bradley*! Fetch us some water, please." They both waited for a response from Bradley. Walter snorted again when there was none. Several seconds later, though, Bradley entered with two glasses of water and a green, glass bottle. After Bradley poured some of the bottle's contents into Philip's glass, he took it and gingerly held it in his lap. He had never seen water with bubbles in it before.

"Go ahead, drink," Walter said.

Philip took a sip. The carbonation along with the slight bitterness made his lips pucker. "Do people call you sir?"

"Please, no. My cousin was the only person in our family who commanded that type of respect. I've just inherited an estate, and I have a pompous last name." Philip heard Bradley shuffle past, but could not see him because of the darkness in the hallway outside of the study.

"I try not to pry, largely because I do not appreciate prying myself. However, I felt quite a reaction in you when Bradley mentioned that your father would be coming to get you from work. Was I correct?"

Philip shimmied his butt back into the seat. "It's fine. He will just be upset."

"Upset, and that's all?"

"Say, how can you tell these things about me, anyway? How puny I am, or my reaction to something someone else said. How can you tell?"

"Philip, when you have lived in darkness for as long as I have, you learn other ways to see your environment. It is but one sense, and a person can either adapt or perish."

"Really? What else can you tell?"

"Oh, that this was not your first stressful situation of the day." Philip couldn't believe the words. "Don't be surprised. The stench of layers of sweat on a person's skin is as potent as a sliced onion."

"It wasn't a great day."

"The girl who left you, was it that?"

"How'd you know about that?"

"Philip, just because my own eyes do not work, does not mean that Bradley's aren't fully functional."

59

"Anyway, no, it wasn't about her. Not really."

Walter's right hand trembled around where the bottle of Perrier should be. He found it and filled his own glass. "More?"

"No, thank you. I still have enough."

Walter stuck the stopper back into the bottle. He folded his hands into a tent and rested his chin on his thumbs. "Do you care to tell me what happened today at school?"

Philip didn't understand this man's interest in what happened to him at school. He also knew that there would be no benefit to telling him. There was nothing Philip felt he needed to get off his chest. To the contrary, he had a feeling of achievement. Taking down his biggest bully and getting away with it.

"No, sir."

Walter parted his hands and rubbed his face. "I understand. I respect your privacy." There was a pounding noise from somewhere within the castle. "Ah, that must be your father."

Philip instantly felt queasy. Somehow, being in the castle had made him feel safe. The protective blanket was about to be ripped off.

"Let's go. Follow me, Philip." They made their way through the dark hallway with pitch-black rooms off the sides. When they arrived at the front door, Bradley was waiting for them.

"It's the boy's father."

Walter snorted. "Go ahead, open the door, Bradley."

Philip watched Bradley slide a tremendously thick, wrought iron bar across the door frame. He tugged on the door to dislodge it, and then opened it while stepping back.

"Philip!" Philip stepped forward with his head down. "What the hell are you doing here?"

"Now, Mr. Sturling, please do not worry. Your young son simply asked for a tour of the castle. It is not something that I frequently allow, but I felt generous with a young man of his intelligence and interest."

Philip looked up at Walter and thought he caught the slightest of smirks.

"Well, Mr . . . umm — I'm afraid I don't know your last name."

"von Richthofen. Walter von Richthofen, the second."

"Okay. Mr. von Richthofen, I am very sorry for the intrusion. I promise this will never happen again," his dad said with a hard pinch of Philip's arm.

"No, no. Anytime Philip is interested, he can come by the Richthofen Castle. Just knock next time," Walter said, this time letting his smile spread.

"Thank you," Philip's father said as he turned and pulled Philip to their car.

* * * * *

It was just under a mile back to their house. Philip wished it would never end. The backseat provided him a temporary refuge from his father's rage. He could see his father's hands gripping the steering wheel with white knuckles. The 1957 Ford Custom dutifully made its way back, unaware that it was carrying out a sentence.

They pulled into the short driveway and Philip waited for his father's order. There was none, just a gruff hand wrenching him from the backseat. His father dragged him up the stairs to the home and fumbled with his keys. The door opened before he could find the right one.

"Oh, my God! Philip, what did you do at school today?!"

"Get out of the damn way, Missie." His father brushed her away and pulled him into the house. He pushed Philip onto the living room couch. "This little truant broke into a house today." A briefcase hit the ground. A cup hit the counter. His dad poured some whiskey out of a bottle.

"What are you talking about?"

"Just what I said, Missie. He broke into a damn house. Why do you think I'm here? The homeowner called me at work and I had to go pick him up."

Another click of the glass hitting the counter verified its contents were drained.

"Well, I just can't believe . . . well, he was . . . he had trouble at school today, too."

Philip knew his mom didn't mean it. He knew she didn't

mean to throw that fuel onto the fire. She was just so wrapped up in her emotions and things came out. She wasn't as sharp as his father. He knew she didn't mean it.

It came out, though. Everything paused. Everything turned motionless and silent.

"Oh, Benjamin, Ben, darling. I thought he told you. Just take a moment. Now, wait!" Hard steps moved in Philip's direction in conjunction with his mom's sentences. All of a sudden, Philip was in the air, hoisted there by his father.

"What did you do today? I'm sick of you! You shit, I'm sick of you!" His father was shaking him. The room jarred in Philip's eyes. His father tucked him under his arm and made for the room.

"Benjamin! Just calm down, please!"

Philip was facing the ground, so he couldn't see his mom running after them. His dad stormed up the steps. When he reached the room, he threw Philip so hard that he slid to the far wall with the window.

"Benjamin!"

"Stay out of here!"

"Benjamin! Philip!" He saw his mom get to the top of the steps. He was surprisingly calm inside. It was as if destiny had revealed itself in this moment. He saw his dad grab a strap from the table.

"This is going to be the end of everything, boy."

His mom ran down the hall, her shoes off. She threw one into the room haphazardly. It struck his dad's shoulder. Timing her steps perfectly, his dad spun around with the back of his forearm and connected with his mom's face. Her head nearly turned all the way around to the back.

"No!! Mom!" Philip sprung up and grabbed an ice pick from the table. His dad's words clanged around in his jostled head. *Do something bad to them.* Only, there was one bully remaining. Charging his dad with what should have been innocent steps, he lunged and planted the pick straight into his chest. There were two tentative coughs. Philip took the pick out and stabbed it back in. Angry creases in his dad's forehead softened, then hardened, then softened. He staggered back a step, looking into Philip's eyes while holding him to his chest.

His father's grip was too tight now and they were too close for Philip to do anything but stab at his back. Another cough, this time a wet one. Then his dad seemed to gain his bearing.

"Philip?" His eyes started to roll into the back of his head. They snapped back. "Philip. You're coming with me."

His dad stumbled forward, holding onto him, and broke through the second-story window.

FIVE

Donald leaned back and rubbed the sides of his head. It was past two in the morning. Rose had been telling them the story of the Sturlings for over four hours now. They spent most of the time slack-jawed, not able to fathom something so terrible taking place in their house.

"They don't have to disclose any of this?" It was the first thing Donald said in over an hour.

"I don't think so, dear. It was so long ago." Rose set her glass down on the coffee table. "I'm sorry to have delivered this news to you. I felt wrong not telling you, you understand?"

"Of course we do, right, Donald?"

He bobbed his head. "Thank you for coming over, Rose. Thank you for spending so much time letting us know about this."

She stood and flattened out her dress with her hands. Her sunken eyes showed fatigue. "This is a late night for me. I don't often stay awake past nine," she said with some levity.

"Oh, believe me, neither do we!" Faith responded.

They escorted her to the door and it closed behind her more heavily than ever before.

Faith gave him a wide-eyed expression. Donald went to the kitchen and poured himself a glass of water.

65

"We can't stay here," she whispered while leaning over the bar.

He clucked his tongue. "What the heck do you mean? Can't stay here? We've just finished unpacking the place."

"You want to stay here knowing all that? Knowing about the Sturlings and what happened here?"

"Listen, that was so long ago."

"How long ago was it that Philip was here, delivering cookies? That isn't enough to raise the hair on your arms? Look, look at my arms. Total chicken meat."

"The fact that he delivered cookies, that in and of itself means he wasn't a ghost. Probably just some random coincidence with a kid in the neighborhood being named that."

"Don! Come on. Don't be the idiot in a horror movie."

He threw his head back and had to laugh. "I'm *not* being the idiot in a horror movie. I'm just not willing to pack up and leave this house that quickly. We knew we were buying an old house, and we knew that something was likely to have happened in it."

"A *murder*? Maybe someone dying or something like that. Not a murder, Don."

He rested a hand on the kitchen counter and leaned on it. His eyes drooped. "I'm tired. Can we talk about this more tomorrow?"

"Do you want to slip into bed and cuddle Philip? Or, how

about Missie?" She grinned at him.

"You're crazy. No, I just want people in this world in the bed tonight. Tomorrow, maybe we'll invite the others."

She pinched his butt as he went past, and he playfully slapped her hand away.

* * * * *

Don slipped out from under the sheets and put his slippers on. He eased off of the bed. Something woke him up, a song playing softly somewhere in the house. After standing there for several seconds, he looked back at Faith lying in the bed. She was asleep with her mouth open, her usual heavy breathing. It was about the only thing she did that wasn't delicate and womanly. And, it was totally out of her control.

He went across the hall and checked in on the girls. They were both sound asleep.

Where the hell is that music coming from?

Maybe he left the stereo in his office playing. A warm glow spilled from the main level.

"Dammit," he muttered. Must have left a light on. He toed the edge of the first stair and then ambled down the rest of them. Clumsy, half-awoken hands rubbed his eyes as he walked around the wall that partially separated the living room from the sitting and eating area of the floor.

The music was louder here. None of the lights were on, but the glow filled the far corner of the floor where the door to the backyard was. Don stopped in his tracks. Any sleepiness in his eyes was instantly erased by adrenaline and fear. He glanced to his left, to the stairs down to the garden level. It was pitch dark down there. None of the glow on this floor escaped down that stairway.

The song kept playing, as if in a loop. It was Roy Orbison. Next thing he knew, he was sitting down on one of the padded benches they had arranged in the sitting room. The room was brighter, lit by the normal lights in the room rather than the warm glow of before. Faith was in the kitchen. The girls were seated at the dining room table. He called out to Faith, but it was as if a gulf in between them sucked away the sound.

"Faith, dammit, what are you doing?" This time, she looked up and smiled. Something was wrong with her face though. She held the smile almost as if her skin was pinned there. Then, she released it and looked back down to the food she was preparing.

Don shook his head. Something caught his eye, something above him. He looked up at the ceiling fan. The blades weren't moving. The pull for the light was hanging normally. The pull for the fan blades was extended out to a forty-five degree angle, and it just stayed there. His stomach dropped. He yelled out to Faith. She looked up with that smile again. He tried to get up but he was immobilized. The song got louder. That's when he recognized it. That's when the girls looked at him with the same smile as their mother.

Next thing, he was in his bed. Faith was shaking him.

"Don . . . Don!" The fuzzy edges of reality started to harden. "Don, you're having a dream. A dream, Don. A dream."

THE ROOM

The music came back to him from her words. Dream, dream, dream. Roy Orbison. The collar of his T-shirt was soaked. His back was soaked. He sat straight up and looked at Faith.

"Honey, it was just a dream."

69

SIX

The bell rang, sending the students into a frenzy to gather their things and get out of the classroom. Brooke waited impatiently by the door while Charity took her time to make sure she had everything she needed.

"Come on, Charity!" Brooke bounced up and down.

"Let's go, Charity," Mrs. Sachs echoed.

"Hold on, I just want to make sure I have everything to do my homework."

Mrs. Sachs smiled and gave Brooke a knowing look. Brooke huffed and turned out of the classroom.

"Okay, okay I'm coming!" Not being one to break into a complete sprint, Charity fast-stepped it to catch up to Brooke.

"You're so slow," Brooke said once Charity was a couple feet behind her. Charity ignored the comment and tightened the left shoulder strap on her backpack. Brooke made a face at a couple of girls she didn't like and motored out of the swinging doors to the street.

"Why'd you do that?" This time, Brooke ignored Charity.

It was sunny out, but still chilly. Charity untied the sweater from her waist and stopped to put it on. Brooke didn't bother to turn around. Once Charity was done, Brooke resumed her relentless march.

"Why are you walking so fast?" Brooke turned right and headed up the hill on Richthofen Place. "Brooke, where are you going?"

"I want to take a longer walk today."

"But, it's supposed to start snowing in a couple of hours."

Brooke stopped. "How do you know the weather?" she asked with her eyebrows squeezed together. "You're a kid, what kid knows the weather?"

"Mom said it this morning."

"You're so weird." Brooke started up again. "I'm just taking a longer walk. You can come with me or not." Brooke knew who she was dealing with. No way would Charity walk home alone. Their parents forbade that, and it would be a more significant transgression than taking a longer walk.

"Okay, okay." Charity tucked her hands into the pockets of her sweater and this time ran a few steps to catch up. "How far?"

"Just a few blocks."

Charity looked at her sister and instantly knew something was up. It was the intuition that only two people who had shared a womb could have. At the same time, she knew that if she pressed for more details, Brooke would just stonewall and tease her.

A brisk wind gusted up and blew their skirts against their knees as they trudged up the hill. They reached the top and Brooke looked from right to left.

71

"I knew you didn't know where you're going."

"I didn't get exact directions."

"Directions? From who?"

Brooke pointed to something above the horizon. "There!"

Charity followed her sister's finger and saw something that looked like the spire of a castle. "What is that?"

Brooke double-timed it until she stood in front of two towering gates.

Charity shook her head. "Did you know this was here?"

"Not until Philip told me."

Charity grabbed Brooke's backpack. "Brooke! We said we weren't going to talk to him anymore. Not after what we heard Ms. Rose tell Mom and Dad."

"Well, how can I stop him if he wants to talk to me? I can't kick him out of the house, can I?"

That stumped Charity. "What did he tell you?"

"He told me that this castle was here. He told me that a nice old man lives in it. So, I wanted to see it."

"Okay, we've seen it." The windows on this side of the castle had curtains that creeped out Charity. She wanted to be gone.

Brooke pushed on the gate and it gave way. She turned her head to Charity and smiled. "See, it's meant to be."

"No way, Brooke. No way! We'll get into so much trouble."

"From who? Who's going to know?"

"No way. I'm going home."

"Have it your way." Brooke slipped through the gate and slowly made her way down a dirt path to the front doors of the castle. Charity stood paralyzed outside of the gate. She watched as Brooke reached the big, wood front doors. She saw Brooke try one of them out, and then again a bit harder. They didn't give. Brooke made her way around the perimeter of the castle until she was about to move out of Charity's sight.

"Brooke!" Charity whispered as loud as she could. Brooke's head snapped around and she gave Charity a nasty look. Charity stepped between the gate and the stone column and took the same path as Brooke, almost like she expected any different step to lead her to a different fate. Brooke waited for her, a grin as big as a slice of watermelon on her face.

"The front door wouldn't open."

"What did you expect, it to be open for you? This isn't a movie. People live here, Brooke."

"I'm going to look for another door. There has to be another."

"Oh, my gosh, we're going to be in so much trouble."

"Stop being a baby."

They made their way around the castle in silence until they came to a wood enclosure buried into the ground. It had two doors that were latched closed. There was no lock on the latch. Brooke glanced at Charity.

"No way!" Charity hissed.

Brooke paused. "Okay, this time you're right. That's just too scary."

They continued around the side of the castle. Piles of rusted junk lay dying behind the castle, invisible to passersby.

"I don't like it, Brooke."

Brooke continued around the back wall of the castle, glued to its facade. They came to a door.

"Here," Brooke said. She tried the door, but it was locked. "No!"

"We've tried. Let's go. Someone is going to come home soon, Brooke."

"We're in here, we can't just turn back now." Brooke pressed her nose against the glass in the door. "It's so dark inside, I can't see anything."

Brooke moved away from the door and started to walk back to the side of the castle.

"Thank you, Lord," Charity sighed.

Charity tiptoed while Brooke let her feet fall heavily. They came to the wood enclosure and Brooke stopped.

"No, even you said it was too scary."

"There's no other way in."

"That's because people live here and they've locked their house! That's normal!"

Brooke flipped the latch back.

"Brooke, you don't even know if we can get in through there!"

"There's only one way to find out." Brooke flung back one of the wood doors. It was surprisingly clean, like it had been used recently. "Hmm, I expected some cobwebs." She grabbed Charity's hand and dragged her into the cellar.

There was a short corridor with a low ceiling and then a wood door with a glass center. The corridor wasn't anything like the girls expected. It wasn't damp. It wasn't creepy at all, really. In fact, it seemed to be used frequently. Brooke could feel Charity's tension release a little through her hand.

"Okay, okay, let's go," Charity said.

The door in the corridor was slightly ajar. Brooke pulled it open and stepped through. Her skirt caught on the rough edges of the opening. They stepped into a room lit only by a flickering light in the far corner. This room was freezing, almost like cold air was being forced into it.

"What's this?"

"I don't know," Charity answered as she edged her way around the perimeter of the room. Once they reached the far wall, they could see that the whole wall was lined with floor-to-ceiling shelves.

Brooke grabbed something off one of the shelves. "It's a can." She wiped the label clean with her forearm. "Peaches." She grabbed a couple more and performed the same wipe-down. All of the cans contained some sort of food.

"A food cellar."

"Yeah."

They moved on toward the light. It stopped flickering when they stood under it.

"Brooke."

Brooke grabbed her hand and squeezed it. "I saw."

They came to another door, totally different than the first one. This one was solid, and when Brooke knocked on it lightly, they could both tell it was metal. Brooke leaned on it and tried to push the door, but it didn't give at all. Brooke could hear the relief in Charity's breathing.

"You've had your fun, let's go now," she whispered.

"I want to explore more."

"Brooke, there's nowhere else to go! We've sneaked into someone's home. Let's go!"

Much like her earlier pleas, this one died in the synapses of Brooke's mind. "Give up" were words that simply did not register with her.

"Why would you leave the door from the outside open, but then lock this one? That doesn't make sense."

"Maybe the people don't care about food getting stolen, but they don't want people inside the actual house. It makes *perfect* sense to me, Brooke."

Brooke examined the door. There was no latch on the inside. It was completely smooth and entirely disheartening. After several minutes, Brooke sighed and sat with a huff, her back against the door.

"See, I told you."

The light flickered again, and Brooke felt herself start to fall backwards. The door was open a crack.

"No, see, I told *you*," Brooke said self-righteously.

"That's not funny. That door opened when the light flickered."

"Someone wants us to come in. It's good news!" Brooke shot up from the floor and pushed on the door. This time, it groaned open, its metal hinges bound by time, moisture, and neglect.

Behind the door was a stairwell with a wrought iron banister. Again, the only light was at the top of the stairs, providing little illumination. The pupils of their eyes had adjusted to the low light by now though, and they saw everything in a grainy, gray palate.

Brooke climbed the stairs, which were cut differently than normal stairs. The girls both had to use the banister to provide them extra leverage as their short, skinny legs crested each monster-sized stair. Huffing and puffing at the top of the stairs, Brooke stopped and waited for Charity to catch up.

"Those stairs are *not* normal!"

"I know, they are so big." Charity saw a change come over Brooke's face, and they both stopped their labored breathing. They stared into each other's eyes, trying to figure out where that sound came from. Charity shook her head, her eyes wide and her lips pressed tightly together. Nothing else happened for several seconds and Charity shrugged her shoulders.

Another door greeted them. This one was much less imposing than the one out of the food cellar. Brooke turned the handle slowly and tried to slide the door open as quietly as possible. Decades would not be undone quietly, however, and it screeched like an owl as it rotated through part of its arc. Brooke turned sideways and squeezed through as small of an opening as she could.

Now, they were in the house. A long hallway led to what appeared to be the front of the house. Light fought its way through stained glass on either side of the front door. It was a world away, as several open rooms lined both sides of the hallway. Brooke whisked Charity through the door and shut it.

Their chests were rising and falling dramatically. Being in the actual living space of the castle changed the feeling. It was completely dark save for the area near the front door. To their left was a long, rectangular room with many oversized chairs in it. To their right was a dining room. The table was completely set, and various hutches lined the room with fine china on display.

They heard the noise again. This time, they were able to identify it more clearly. Something low and guttural. It seemed to come from the dining room, and it sent them scurrying into the rectangular room. Shortly after they did, a door swung open to the dining room. A person, difficult to distinguish as a shorter man or woman, came through hurriedly. It began dusting one of the hutches and then stopped.

The girls each crouched behind a chair, their quadriceps burning from holding the position so firmly. They peeked out to see the person go to the door they had just come through and grab the knob. It stood there, as if gathering information just from touching the house. Then, it went back into the dining room and started dusting another hutch. It made its way to all of the hutches, four in all, and was headed back to the door it came through when it stopped again. This time, it turned with such speed that it almost could not be defined as movement. Both girls caught their breath. It was looking right at them. Then, they heard the guttural sound again. This time it was louder, and from directly behind them.

Charity took off shrieking for the front door. Brooke followed her. Charity fumbled with the handle. Brooke noticed a thick, metal bar drawn across the door. She pushed it back and got the door open. They both streaked across the front yard and to the gate where they had snuck in. Once out, Brooke stopped and looked back at the castle. All of the curtains remained still. No silhouette appeared in a window. She smiled and they headed home.

* * * * *

Don stood in the doorway. The original blood-red door to the house matched his current emotions. It was twelve past four o'clock and the girls still weren't home from school. A ball of anger grew in his stomach every five minutes that passed without their arrival. Faith had already called the school, called the police, and driven around the neighborhood. The police told them that if the girls didn't show up by five-thirty, or two hours after school let out, that they would start the process of a missing persons investigation.

He tapped the side of his arms with his fingers. Cars whisked past, a teeming sea of faces checked out and on auto-pilot. Don felt like someone was behind him and thought he saw a shadow from the corner of his eye. He turned his head, expecting to see Faith there. There was no one and nothing there, though. Before he could think about it more, he heard quick, rasping footsteps coming down the sidewalk to their house.

The girls already sported concerned looks on their faces, but those looks turned worse when they saw Don standing at the top of the stairs to the front door. Charity immediately started crying. Brooke smiled and screamed, "Daddy!" Her attempt to brush aside the situation infuriated Don more.

He pushed the front door open and stood to the side. "Get the fuck inside."

"Don!"

He ignored Faith. When the girls were right at the door, he pushed them both inside.

"Daddy!" Brooke yelled.

"Don't Daddy me! Where the hell have you been?" He slammed the front door shut and stalked the girls to the kitchen. "Stop right now!"

The girls stopped in their tracks. Faith tried to grab his arm but he shrugged her off. Even Brooke's face was showing signs of cracking. Her normal, tilted grin was gone. Don could see her hands shaking as she tried to stabilize them by grabbing onto her skirt.

"Where have you been?"

Charity was of no use. Her chin was on her chest, which was heaving faster than she could breathe.

"Brooke, where have you two been?" Faith asked calmly.

Don ripped his tie off and threw it onto the dining room table.

"We just took a long walk."

"A long walk?"

"Mommy, Daddy is scaring me," Brooke said.

"You better be scared. You know how scared we were?!" Don saw something out of the corner of his eye again. "Dammit."

"Don, come over here." Faith went back by the front door. He reluctantly followed. "I've never seen you act like this."

"They've never done anything like this," he hissed.

"You're scaring them! You're overreacting." She glanced over his shoulder and he moved his head to block her view. This made her furrow her eyebrows.

"They *need* to be scared."

Faith crossed her arms. "Now, you're scaring me. Please go outside and cool off."

He stared at her until she walked away. Don could hear Faith whispering to the girls, and they scampered upstairs. Turning around, he saw Faith leaning on the kitchen counter. Then, he caught a better glimpse of what he had been seeing before. A shadow, more like mist, rose from her far side and then disappeared. It was visible enough to know that it was there, but also quick enough to cause him to question himself. He rushed out of the front door and gulped air.

SEVEN

Don's mom and Faith made polite conversation on the way home from the airport. She was a professor of mathematics at Ohio State University and her husband was a stockbroker before they both hung it up. There wasn't much room in their house for fantasy or miracles or any of the other nonlinear, unexplainable things that provided the foundation for belief in religion. So, when Don broke it to them that he was marrying someone named Faith, and that they would be having their wedding in the Presbyterian Church, both she and her husband were disappointed. It wasn't the end of the world, like if Don hadn't finished college. But, they knew there would be uncomfortableness between them, Faith, and her family forever.

For these first eleven years of their son's marriage, they effectively avoided any conversations or topics that may even broach religion. However, with the girls at an age that religion was an important topic, and an unavoidable one at that, cracks were starting to manifest in the brittle facade built between their families. Renee believed, too, that those same stresses had to exist between Don and Faith to some degree.

They arrived at the house just before dinnertime. It had been a long day for Renee. Her gray and white hair, the mane of the feminist, fanned out from shoulder to shoulder. She took a moment to breathe in some of the fresh Colorado air to relax. There was no doubt she always had a tendency to be the professor — stern and cold. She made the mistake of raising Don in that environment. It was something she regretted to this day. She promised herself she would never make the same mistake with the girls.

"Very nice, Faith," she said while taking a first look at the house. It was constructed of brick all the way up to the top floor, where the brick exterior ended and the Tudor stucco finish started. She glanced across the street and saw smoke rising from one of several chimney stacks in the neighbor's house. Faith handed her the carry-on bag and they walked along the north side of the house to the steps leading to the front door.

"Nona!!" Renee looked up and saw the twins standing in front of the door, their arms crossed and their hands clutched against their sides. "Hurry up, Nona! It's cold!"

She smiled and broke composure for a moment, yanking the rolling bag up the stairs with a big smile on her face. "My girls! Get inside before you catch something." She made it through the door and knelt down to embrace them. They each took one of her sides and kissed the sides of her face. After a prolonged hug, Renee pulled back. "Let me see you two girls. Or, should I say ladies?"

This made them both smile wildly. "Girls, Nona!" Charity said. She looked at Charity softly. The girl was vastly different from herself. The innocence and tenderness of Charity was a foil to Renee's personality. Brooke, on the other hand, was cut from the same cloth as Renee. She smacked Brooke on the butt and asked what trouble she had gotten into lately. Brooke smiled ruefully and let Charity enjoy their Nona's love. Renee stood up and removed her tan overcoat. Don obligingly took it from her and gave her a brief kiss on the cheek.

"Well, Mom, what do you think?"

She looked around, taking the house in for the first time. "This floor is very open, that's wonderful." The more she looked

84

though, the more the dilapidated state of the house screamed out. It was clear that Faith had tried to place rugs, furniture, and wall art in strategic places, but that couldn't hide everything.

Renee walked around a small wall to the kitchen. A strange mix of upgraded cabinets and countertops intermingled apologetically with walls painted copper and a cheap-looking, raised bar area.

"There's a lot of work to still be done," Don said.

"Oh, nothing some paint won't take care of." She knew the false optimism wouldn't fly with Don, but she didn't do it for him. He knew the score. "You've always been handy, Don."

"Courtesy of your dad." She smiled.

Parts of the rest of the house were in a more startling state of disrepair than the main floor. The garden level was in terrible condition, with bubbling in the paint on the walls that surely indicated some form of mold or water intrusion. The basement was carpeted, but Renee almost felt like her shoes were getting dirty just from walking down there. She kept her poker face on while she took the tour, and while she saw the twins run around each room that they visited.

They headed upstairs next, and the bedroom level was at least in a livable state. Although, the paint in the girls' bedroom was a gaudy pink. Perhaps a prior owner had used this room for a little girl. Blue painters tape still lined the edges of the wall, as if someone had been run out of the house in the middle of the painting project. Finally, they took her up to the finished attic, which was shaped like a long rectangle. Part of it was newly refinished with paint and carpet, and then furnished with the girls' toys and books. Heading the other way was a corridor to a solid-looking door. Renee started to head that way, despite the feeling just looking at the door immediately gave her.

Don put a hand on her shoulder, surprisingly firm. "That's just the space I'm using as an office. Nothing in there yet, really." She stopped and looked back at him, the natural creases in her face expressing everything she needed to express. "You're probably hungry, right?"

She nodded and they headed back to the main level, which seemed like a respite from the rest of the house.

"You have work to do here for years," she said as Faith prepared dinner.

Faith rolled her eyes. "Tell me about it. But, we fell in love with the house the first time we saw it. We couldn't pass up the opportunity."

"So, it was in foreclosure?"

"Yes," Don answered.

"That may explain why it seems someone rushed out of here."

"And, why things like light fixtures and switch plate covers were taken. The house certainly had a strange feeling," he said.

"Don, how on earth will you have time to fix this house up?"

"It'll be a mix of me and contractors, Mom. We'll get it done."

"You got a good price on it, I assume?"

"Very good."

"Well, that's nice then."

Faith called for the girls to come to the table, and they bounded in shrieking and laughing. Charity gave Renee another hug and then sat down at the table.

"Nona, when are you and Poppa going to move out here?"

"Oh, my dear, we're already working on it."

"We want you close!" the girls yelled in unison. Then they giggled.

Renee enjoyed Faith's excellent cooking and then the bustle of the day started to set into her muscles. Her fatigue must have been apparent to Don and Faith, because they almost simultaneously asked her if she wanted to turn in for the night. She said she did, and Don grabbed her bag as she headed for the basement bedroom. Renee wasn't one to be squeamish at all, but being set up in a cold, dirty basement wasn't at the top of her bucket list.

Don could read her like an open book, something she knew he had developed after years of walking on eggshells around her.

"Mom, I'm sorry about the state of things. If you want to stay at a hotel instead, just let me know and I'll pay for it."

"Donald, you know it's not about money. I'll be just fine here. The sheets are at least clean, right?"

Don crossed his arms. "We figured you wouldn't mind the sheets that the last owner left."

She threw him a look that basically told him to go to hell, but then smiled. "I'll be fine. I'll just close my eyes and it will be morning." He smiled back and then turned and left the room.

"Good night, Mom," he called out.

"Good night," she whispered back.

She dropped her carry-on suitcase onto the bed and unzipped it. After digging for and finding her toiletry bag, she headed for the bathroom on the garden level. The sink was about the only thing that didn't look terrible. There was no mirror, so she just pulled out her wipes and started removing makeup from her face.

I can't believe my grandchildren live in this, she thought. She put the wipe on the side of the sink. There wasn't a trashcan either. She pulled out her toothbrush and gingerly turned on the water. For a moment she expected something brown or red to come oozing out. To her surprise, regular-looking water came out.

"Well, that's a miracle."

She let water run over the toothbrush before putting toothpaste on it and then started to mechanically move it around her mouth. Something glimmered in the corner of her eye. It was almost like a light quickly shined onto a mirror from an angle. The toothbrush stopped in her mouth. To her right was an old window, tall and slim with obscured glass. Behind her was the old cast iron bathtub. Nothing else that she could see. It wasn't altogether out of the ordinary for her old eyes to play tricks on her.

She restarted brushing, trying to remember what area of her mouth she had stopped at. Then, she saw it again. This time it was definite, likely caught because she was still on alert. It was a glimmer, something that shot across the wall above the window; as fleeting and yet as concrete as a passing thought.

Strangely, the feeling she got was not scared. Rather, it was calm. It was almost like the temperature in the room increased to something comfortable, entirely bearable. Something rasped in the bathtub behind her. She spun around, the toothbrush stuck in the back of her mouth.

"Hello?"

Now, she absolutely had the feeling that someone was in there with her. For an entirely rational, logic-based person, this was a new experience. For someone who wholeheartedly refused to believe in any deity, any spiritual world, she was now confronted with something beyond logical explanation.

"Hello?"

When the response came, it sounded like something sucked air in from the room first. It was a high-pitched voice, a child's, that said "hello" back to her.

She had always speculated regarding this moment, particularly since becoming older. Once the specter of age and death became something she could not shove aside. Once the truest part of her existence sat in front of her, changing position no matter which way she looked. Renee had speculated about a moment when she would be confronted with something other than numbers and formulas. It wasn't nearly as terrifying as she had expected.

She went over to the tub and touched it. It was oddly warm.

"Hello? Who are you?"

The same sound preceded the same answer. "Hello." It sounded almost like a recording. The idiolect of some child ghost captured on cassette tape. Something in the voice turned Renee tender. The fact that it seemed lost.

"Darling, where are you?"

"Momma?"

Renee sat down on the bathroom floor. Just as she did, the air-sucking sound started again but then stopped. The light overhead flickered and the room instantly turned cold.

"Hello, my dear, are you still there?"

She heard something garbled, but extremely deep and aggressive. Renee thought about getting up. Her mind registered the intent, but nothing was communicated to the rest of her body. Frozen to the floor, she started to feel what she had initially expected. Terror, fear, depression. The warmth ran from the room as quickly as a whipped horse. Her eyes widened as wave after wave of emotion hit her, compressing her chest. There were no images in front of her eyes, just the bare bathroom, but awash in a different light than anything man-made. Her head tilted to the side under the pressure of the control.

Another deep grunt and the temperature started to rise in the bathroom again. The vise grip around her body loosened. Renee started to cry, out of her own fear, but also for the terror and depression that she just experienced. She hadn't cried since childhood. Not even when her children were born. She wept decades of tears until she could weep no more. Then, she quickly gathered her things, stuffed them into her suitcase, and woke Donald to take her to a hotel.

* * * * *

"Philip told me that isn't true," Brooke whispered to her sister. "He told me that Grandma left because she was scared, not because she was sick."

The girls were in their bedroom. They sat on the floor, Indian-style.

"Scared of what?"

Brooke tilted her head to the side. "You know."

"You know there's nothing like that, Brooke! You know it's the power of . . ."

"Oh, stop that God *crap*."

"Hey, I'm going to tell Mom you said a bad word."

"Go ahead. Besides, if you believe in God, then don't you believe in all the evil they teach us about?"

"I *do* believe in God."

"When's the last time you saw him, Charity?"

They heard footsteps and the door opened. "Girls, what are you doing up here?" their grandma asked.

"Nothing," they replied in unison. She smiled and stepped out of the room while pulling the door shut.

Brooke looked back at Charity. "Well?"

"I see him all the time, Brooke. You just can't see Him because you don't want to."

"I don't see Him because He isn't here. You can't believe in just the good part, Charity."

"I do believe the bad . . . but, I don't believe that's here."

"You've seen Philip!"

"But, I don't think he's evil."

Brooke slid closer to Charity on her butt. She put her mouth to Charity's ear. "You've seen *it*."

Charity yanked her head back. "No, I haven't!"

"You've felt it and heard it." This time, Charity was silent. "*I've* seen it."

"What?!"

Brooke just nodded her head and went over to their piles of dolls. She pointed to the middle of the pile.

"In here."

"That's enough, Brooke!"

Brooke saw her sister start to get teary and knew it was time to reel it back. No sense in having Charity spill the beans because she had to go cry to their parents.

"Look, all I'm saying is that there's something here. Have you ever seen Grandma get scared?" Charity shook her head. "Grandma is usually the *scary* one!"

Suddenly, the door opened. They hadn't heard any footsteps and it startled both of them. Their dad stood there. Then he stepped through and closed the door behind him.

"What are you two doing?"

The girls looked at each other. There was something strange in his eyes, something they both picked up on instantly. One of the dolls fell off of the top of the chair behind Brooke.

"Just playing, Daddy," Brooke responded.

"Don't lie to me. I can hear what you're talking about."

"But . . ."

"There's *nothing* in this house. Stop being such scaredy-cats."

"Well, what happened to Grandma then?" Brooke asked in a defiant tone.

Her dad smiled. "She didn't feel well and didn't want to get sick in our house. You heard that when you were eavesdropping on the conversation, didn't you?" Brooke looked down. "That's what I thought."

He stood up. "Now, I want you two to stop this nonsense about the house." With that, he left the room.

Brooke saw Charity's shoulders start to shudder. She went over to her sister, sat behind her, and put two delicate arms around her neck.

EIGHT

Don tried to match Faith's rushed steps. He couldn't believe what she had just said.

"Hold on, Faith, you can't leave now." They walked ahead of the girls to a local grocery store. She didn't respond and her face remained steadfast. "Seriously, it's *Christmas*."

"It's only for a few weeks, Don," she whispered back to him as they stopped to wait for the girls to catch up.

"How is this even right?" Don asked her.

"The girls need a break. They've been holed up for months while we bust our *butts* to get this house into a livable state."

"Three weeks? I've never been away from them for more than three days."

"You'll be fine."

"*No*, you're not taking my daughters." Just as he said it, Don realized how threatening of a posture he was in. Eyes lowered, shoulders angled forward.

"I *am* taking the girls," Faith answered, obviously trying to rebut his own aggression. "Look at you. You want me to tell you the truth? The girls are scared."

He glanced over her shoulder and waited to respond while a patron pushed a squeaky cart out of the store. "Scared? Of this old house?" he hissed.

95

"Of you, Don. They're scared of you. We all need a break."

"We all?"

"Yeah, Don, me too. You're so short-tempered and aggressive lately. You've never been like this. That whole incident of swearing at the girls when they came home late?"

"We thought the girls were *lost* or *kidnapped*."

The girls were right behind them now. They both stopped and Faith asked the girls to take the shopping cart to start filling up from her list. Once they were out of earshot, Don held her arm and started back up.

"So, is this a separation? Some precursor to divorce?"

"No," she said, pulling her arm out of his hand. "Like I said, it's just a break. Three weeks. Then we're back and recharged." She slid a piece of unruly hair back behind her ear. He knew that move. It was uncertainty.
"Where are you guys going?"

"To my parents' house."

"That's a fourteen-hour drive away."

"I know, Don. We're going and not seeing each other for three weeks. Period."

"Dammit, Faith. You're going to force me to do something here."

96

"You don't need to do anything."

"I'm pretty sure I've got rights with those girls too."

"You should just leave it alone, Don. This is a hiatus. I'm not taking the girls to some other country."

He took a deep breath in, contemplating the steps that would be necessary to get some sort of injunction. As a civil trial lawyer, he had no experience or even knowledge of the procedures applicable in family court.

"If you do this, you wouldn't be against me taking the girls for a three-week hiatus either, right?"

"It depends. Isn't that what you tell me a lawyer always says?"

With those parting words, passive aggression embodied, Faith went into the store. Don sighed and wiped his forehead. A black man was sitting on the bench outside of the grocery store. He wore a blue hat with gold embroidery and the name of a Navy ship on it. He had big, plastic glasses and ran his lower jaw back and forth as they walked up. Don's attention shifted to the man from Faith.

"Ain't it a bitch," the man said.

"Sure is. You heard all that?"

"Sure did."

"Little cold out here, don't you think?" he said.

The jaw stopped its shifting. Big, blood-red eyes rolled up to meet Don's voice. "You got a house for me?" he rasped.

"Well, no," Don chuckled abashedly. "But, do you need something warm to eat?"

"How 'bout something warm to drink?"

"Sure. Coffee sound good?"

It was the man's turn to chuckle. "How 'bout some whiskey. That real warm stuff."

Don shook his head. They had a whole cast of homeless people living around their house. With the Navy hat and his generally clean appearance, Don hadn't pegged this man as one of them.

"Sorry, sir, can't do that."

"Say, those your girls just run in?"

Don's tone changed from accommodating to protective. "Don't worry about them."

"I ain't," the man said, his jaw jutting back and forth several times. "But, you should be."

"What's that supposed to mean?"

"Them twins, I seen them up at that corner house of yours." Don felt the hair on the back of his neck bristle. He got a little bit lightheaded, caught off guard by this man. "I seen them up by the castle too."

Don knelt down and got closer. Now, the man was more smell than sight.

"Are you stalking my daughters?"

"Hell, no," the man said with a weak smile. "The booze interests me, not no little girls. I seen them up there 'cause I'm all around this place. They been seeing a little boy. Heard them talk 'bout him. Figured their dad would want to know that, is all." The man's jaw started up again, as did his hands this time. They worked each other over slowly and forcefully.

"Do you know the boy's name?" Don asked.

The man shook his head. "No name. Just ain't right for no young girls like that to be running with no boys. That's what you should be worried 'bout."

Don stood back a little. "Well, thanks for letting me know." He took a five-dollar bill out of his wallet and handed it to the man, then headed into the store. The door chimed when he opened it. He caught up to Faith and the girls in the coolness of the dairy aisle.

Faith leaned into him, "What was that all about?"

Don watched the girls, who were watching him back. "He said the girls were talking about some boy," Don answered, loudly enough for the girls to hear him. "Any idea what that's about?" he directed to them.

They both shook their heads. "We've never seen that old man before," Brooke volunteered.

"That's not what I asked."

"No boys, Dad."

He gave them a long once-over and then pulled them to his sides. "Good, because you know boys are no good, right?" They nodded. "You know they're all smelly and dirty, except for your dad, right?" Now, the girls started to grin. They nodded more aggressively. "And, Daddy's got a surprise for any of them that try to talk to you two." He said this with a deadpan face, which made their smiles disappear. Then he smiled and tousled their hair. They laughed and ran off down the aisle while yelling to Faith they would get the bread.

"Are they really this age already? Can't they just get back on the bottle and in the crib again?"

Don's smile faded with each running step the girls took away from them. "I don't like it at all, Faith."

"You're not changing my mind, Don. This is what's best for the family."

Brooke whipped around a corner with something in her hands and shoved it right into Don's stomach. He winced, but managed a smile.

"No chips, Brooke!" Faith exclaimed.

Don held up the crushed bag. "We bought them now," he mustered to say through the anger percolating from Faith's decision.

* * * * *

Don was in the house again and like in all the dreams, everything was dead silent. Everything was fuzzy, as if the world around him was being gently shaken. There were moments of clarity. Then he would be moving somewhere else in the house.

He recently noted he was the only one in these dreams. Before, he would move through the dreams, through the house and around his family unnoticed. They were nowhere to be found now. No matter what room he went into. Not even a sign that they had been there.

A blur and then he was up in the hallway leading to the room. But, it was different from their house. The walls were charcoal grey. A faint light glowed around the door to the room. Something called him this time. Not using sound. Instead, something pulled at his energy. It was simultaneously terrifying and captivating. He flowed to the door and opened it.

The room was darker than the hallway, but his eyes needed no adjusting. Something brushed along his back and then he made out what looked like a steel door on the wall to his right. The door was small and low. Maybe three-feet high by three-feet wide. As he looked at the door, a cold feeling started to creep up from his feet. It spread to his legs and before he knew it, it had overtaken his entire body. His lungs didn't work. His mouth and eyes were frozen open. The door slammed open at an otherworldly speed. Then, something flew out, too fast for him to really see.

It shocked him awake and he gasped for air as if it was his last before succumbing to drowning. Sweat clammed up the back of his neck and made his T-shirt stick to his body. Both of his hands were pressed into the bed. He gritted his teeth and rubbed them back and forth. Faith was still asleep next to him. He fell back into the pillows with a sigh and rolled over to lay alone on his side of the bed.

NINE

Everything was packed up and the car was loaded. Faith gave him a long hug, but no kiss. The girls wrapped themselves around his legs.

"Daddy, we're going to miss you."

He heard the words like they were from an unseen part of a cave. "I'll miss you too," was all he could manage. Then, they were in Faith's car pulling out into the street. He caught a glimpse of the girls straining their necks to see him. The car turned down a street and they were gone.

Don turned around and trudged back into the house. The silence felt like a trash compactor closing around him. He poured a whiskey and Coke and then went to his office to try to get some work done. He spent most of the time staring out of the window to the backyard below.

"I can't do this."

He picked up his phone and noticed it had only been forty-five minutes since his family left. Shaking his head, he dialed Steve Lischek. Steve was a friend of just about ten years now. They met in law school.

"What's going on, man?"

"Family's gone."

"Ah, hell. Can I ask you a question now that this shit is for real?"

Don braced himself. He never knew what would come out of Steve's mouth. No one did.

"Sure."

"Is this a separation, or just a vacation?"

"A hiatus."

"Yeah, I don't know what the hell that means. It seems to me if Faith had actually called this a separation, you coulda done anything you wanted. Know what I mean? If she's just calling this a hiatus, then I think she's trying to get the best of both worlds. Leave you, and keep you locked down at the same time."

Steve was a forty-two-year-old bachelor. Self-professed addict of women, partying, and the single life. A seasoned patent litigation attorney who worked hard and played even harder. He probably made double the salary Don did.

"Not thinking about that part, Steve."

"Yet. You're not thinking about it yet. First thing you did was call brother Steve, huh?"

Steve had a point there. "You're right. I should have called my mom first."

"Christ, listen to yourself. You're a grown man. We deal with situations like this in the most sophomoric way possible."

Don braced himself again. "How's that?"

"Drinking beer."

"What's the punch line?"

"Drinking beer at a strip club."

"Oh, come on. They've only been gone for an hour."

"You may only get this chance once in your life. Two kids, a wife, all of 'em gone. You tell me all the time, man. You haven't had a breather since we've known each other."

Don stood up and pinched the phone between his ear and his shoulder. He opened the window in front of his desk to let some fresh air in. To hopefully wash away the senselessness of Steve's suggestion.

"I knew I should have called my mom first."

Steve laughed through a cough.

* * * * *

They arrived at her parents' house midafternoon the day after leaving. Faith wanted to make it in one fell swoop, but fourteen hours straight was impossible with the girls. A potty break at least every two hours. Food stops. Photo stops. She gave up four hours in and just got a hotel room once it was time for dinner.

"Faith!" she saw her mom mouth before she stepped out of the car. It was completely typical for her mom to have waited by the window for them to arrive.

"Girls, get your cheeks ready."

"Oh, no!" they moaned in unison.

Her mom had arms and shoulders inside the car like lightning, planting kisses on the girls' cheeks. While Don's mom had the means to visit frequently, her parents didn't. Especially with her father's condition.

Faith let her mom dote on the girls while she went to find her dad. He was sitting in his usual place, the living room next to a radio tuned to an oldies station. The house was disorganized. Her mom had never been a particularly clean person. Add to that the care that her father now needed, and there was no chance for cleanliness.

She put her hands on her father's shoulders. "Dad."

He turned his head and smiled at her. It was the smile that a patient would give a caregiver. He turned his head back to catch the radio waves. She buried her head in his neck and smelled the manliness that had always existed, even as he started and continued to deteriorate on a daily basis.

Faith waited anxiously for the girls to come in. They were the last people he really recognized.

"Grandpa!"

Her dad turned his head slowly. Faith's stomach dropped when she saw his face remain dead, as if being greeted by two strangers. Then, a smile grew on his face.

"Girls," he whispered. "Come here to Grandpa." He opened his wide wingspan of arms and folded the girls into his chest.

"How have you two been?"

The girls launched into a description of school, home, friends, movies, and what phones they wanted for their birthdays. Everything Faith expected of girls their age. Her dad listened contently. His face was placid, unaffected. That was true to his form, and was true even before the Alzheimer's started to set in.

Seeing her dad really did make her miss Don. The men were close. Don was like the son her dad never had. As they grew to know each other, they became friends as only men could be. It was a quiet relationship, filled with fishing, golf, and work around the house when visits could happen. As her father's disease manifested and progressed, she could tell that it was Don he wanted to spend his last coherent days with. Not that he ignored her or her mother, but Don just provided a friendship neither of them ever could.

She could tell that her dad felt something was missing. Faith had an explanation at the ready. "Don is in trial, Dad. He couldn't make this trip."

He nodded his understanding and tuned back into the radio. It was likely that they wouldn't interact with him much more over the course of the trip. There was little left to say to a person that couldn't remember what happened earlier in the day.

Faith's mom was another story. There were times that she thought her dad lost the ability to speak much because her mom took all of it. The downside of coming to her parents' home was that her mom would be relentless in asking about Don. A simple explanation that he was in trial wouldn't be enough. Her mom had the inquisitive paranoia that accompanied a stay-at-home lifestyle.

She didn't wait long to lay in. "How's home life, dear?" Faith shook her head and looked for the girls. "Don't worry," her mother said with a glossy smile, "I looked for them before asking."

"Can't this wait until I take a shower at least?" An old T-shirt was sticking too tightly to her body from the car grime. Blue jeans hugged her legs. They were the wrong choice for the remainder of the drive, but she had grabbed the first thing available to her as she tried to push the girls out of the hotel.

"It's a simple question, dear."

Faith cocked her head, feeling all of the childhood emotions come back to her in a fell swoop. "If I'm here, do you really think it's a simple answer?"

Her mother stopped her fake fussing in the kitchen. The fuss tried to convey that this line of questioning was informal and casual.

"Well, I thought you were here…"

Faith furrowed her eyebrows. "Yes?"

Her mom turned around fully and folded her hands in front of her. "I thought you were here because of your father." Faith remained confused. "You just told us you were coming here, no details."

"Yes. So what does that have to do with Dad?"

"Well, you always had those notions, those premonitions.

Remember?"

Faith rubbed her head. "Mom, you always wanted me to *think* I had some other power of detection. I never did."

"You did this time."

"What do you mean?"

Her mom came and sat down at the kitchen table. She placed her hands on Faith's hands. "Dear, your father is dying."

TEN

Don rubbed his eyes and flipped onto his stomach. It was a beautiful thing to be able to sleep diagonally across the bed. No kids' feet jabbing him in his sides. No wife clinging onto him and making the whole situation too hot. Just as he relished this feeling, a wave of loneliness came over him. He opened his eyes and listened to his breath slip past the pillow. Without its usual occupants, the house was as silent as an empty courtroom.

He pushed the covers off and righted himself, waiting for the lightheadedness and faint stars to clear from his eyes. Unload the bladder. Head downstairs to fill up a glass of orange juice. Don rested an elbow on the raised countertop and wondered if he could manage this kind of lifestyle for any extended period of time. Probably not, he concluded. The whole single thing was way too much effort, with too little upside. Then, to be back in the muck, trying to gladiator your way to the top of some strange woman's list. He laughed at the thought of it and headed up to his office to call the girls.

The usual stairs creaked under the day's new weight. He finished most of the orange juice before he got to the top level and set the glass down on the credenza they had labored to move up to the anteroom. He opened the door to the room, his head down, thinking about what he was going to say to the girls. How he was going to start to rebuild the trust he had damaged with so few words.

A shape, something out of place immediately caught his eye after he opened the door. There was a body slumped in a far corner of the room.

"What in the shit?"

He stood there, his legs suddenly weak. He slammed the door shut and turned around, not sure what to think. The outside world looked normal through the small window at the top of the stairs. Don mumbled something and put a palm on his forehead. Like a dead fish thrown against a wall, he slid down the door and sat in front of it.

The phone rang from inside the room.

"Goddammit." He knew it was probably Faith and the girls calling. He and Faith seemed to have telepathy when it came to calling each other. Even when things weren't going well, neither one of them could stand going too long without hearing from one another.

The phone rang again.

"Coming . . . coming!"

Don braced himself and opened the door. The body was still there. He turned sideways to keep the possibility of a quick retreat open and made his way to his desk. He didn't count how many times the phone rang, but it had reached the point where the next one was likely the last. Don's hand rested on the receiver while he took in the body.

"Hello?"

"Don?"

"Hi, honey," he said emptily.

111

"How are things there?"

The body was female. Blond hair fell to her cheekbones. Blue lips and gray skin almost looked like makeup and contrasted with the vibrancy of her hair.

"Pretty quiet."

"It's a big house."

"Big enough to swallow you up."

There was a pause and then Faith responded, "Yeah."

"You want to talk to the girls?"

"Please."

He heard Faith yell for them and their feet pound as they ran to the phone. The body was in better shape than he would expect something dead to be. The woman's hair was still done up, not disheveled. Her clothes, which looked like club clothes, weren't even wrinkled. Where was the struggle?

"Daddy!"

"Girls," he answered with as much energy as possible.

"Daddy, we miss you. We miss you!"

"I miss you, too." He managed to break out of his one-line responses. "What have you been doing?"

The girls launched into a long explanation of the trip to get to their grandparent's home, then started talking about the fact they were going to the circus tomorrow, and then their words faded along with the world around him. Don knelt down. Voices still migrated through the receiver. He lay down on the floor, the blackness creeping in from the edges of his eyes. Just as the blackness completely overtook his vision, he swore the woman in front of him blinked her eyes.

* * * * *

When Don woke up, the body was still there. Their eyes were on the same level. Her body seemed to be slumped like his. Something about her though seemed to be more alive than even him.

"What the hell?" he muttered. He rubbed his head and slumped over onto a knee. The room was cold. Abnormally cold for being in the attic. The phone beeped consistently until he put it back on the receiver. Suddenly, he felt all the cold in the room coalesce behind him and something ran up his back. The phone rang at the same time and made him spin around in a full circle.

He watched the black, vintage-style phone vibrate in its cradle. It rang again.

"Don?" When he didn't answer, the voice repeated itself, the concern apparent. "Don? You there?"

"Yeah."

"Man, what happened to you last night?"

"Steve."

Steve laughed nervously. "Yeah, man. Steve. You all right?"

Don glanced at the body just a few feet away from him. "Sure."

"Why'd you leave me last night? I went to the bathroom and, boom, you were gone when I got back!"

He pulled the chair out from his desk and sat down. "I don't remember much from last night."

"Well, what do you remember?"

Don searched his memory and rubbed his temple with his free hand at the same time. "To be honest, I don't remember anything."

"Not even that chick sitting on your lap for the last half-hour of the night?"

"No, not even her."

"I'm surprised you didn't go home with her — the way she was eyeing you."

Don paused and formulated his next question carefully. "Sucks. What did I miss?"

"Aw, man, she was a blond, with a haircut like in the '50s. One of those, what do you call it?"

"Pompadour."

"Yeah! Tats. Super slender waist with some perfect tits. Beautiful girl."

The bile rose in Don's throat.

"I need a full picture here, Steve. What was she wearing?"

"Oh, come on, man. I remember stuff from last night, but I was tanked too. Way too tanked to remember what a stripper was wearing in that dark place."

"Yeah, guess it was a dumb question."

"You know, I remember one thing though, 'cause they stood out. She was wearing a pair of Mexican earrings."

"What do you mean?"

"You know, those skull things?"

"Day of the Dead?"

"Yeah, those."

Don leaned closer to the body. "Green."

"Yeah! Green. See, you do remember something. Weird thing to remember."

Don was at a total loss for what to do next. Particularly whether he was going to let Steve in on this. He knew it was probably a stupid thing to even consider. Steve had a big mouth, big ego, all of it. But he felt compelled to tell *someone*. As he was contemplating all of this, the coldness returned to the room. His mind cleared.

"Steve, I gotta go."

"All right, man. But, I'm gonna give you a call later. That strip club messed with your head, for real."

Don hung up. The next steps were perched in front of his eyes like they were written on a chalkboard. He went over to the girl's body and pulled her away from the wall. He looked for blood, bruises—some indication as to how this had happened.

Who are you kidding? Don thought to himself. *You know how this happened.* He slowly put his hands around the girl's neck. A weird feeling came over him. Satisfaction. Like putting the last piece in a puzzle.

"That's it."

He let the body fall back to the wall and headed down to the bedroom. He put on a pair of work jeans, an old T-shirt, and shoes he used to paint in. After putting on a hat from the downstairs closet, he headed out to the local hardware store. All he needed were the canisters of muriatic acid, normally used to clean hardscapes around pools. One of the old garbage cans in the backyard would serve as the container. With a shaky hand, a hand that seemed not his own, he placed the canisters on the checkout counter and paid for the means to destroy another person's body.

After the hardware store, he went to the liquor store and bought a twelve-pack of Coors Light. He thought about it more, and grabbed a case of it. It was going to be a long wait until dusk, and then it was going to be even more work after that.

116

* * * * *

Steve gazed out his window as the news droned on about this afternoon's series of storms. It was raining hard. Lightning was visible and seemed to be closing in on him. He wanted to go check on Don, who had seemed so strange. Steve feared this kind of weather though, dating all the way back to his childhood.

"Screw it, I gotta go."

He put on a pair of jeans and some weatherproof boots. He grabbed a rain jacket from his closet and threw it into the passenger seat of his car as he climbed in. The garage door rattled open, revealing the black sky and driving rain outside. The radio came on and he and selected a classic rock station to calm his nerves.

Steve lived downtown, meaning he had about a twenty-minute drive to Don's house. He didn't call Don to give advanced warning of his visit. Something in him said he needed to catch Don off guard to really see what was going on.

Don was usually a pretty upfront person. That's what made Steve concerned after they finished their phone call. He never knew Don to be evasive, particularly not over something like going to a strip club. Steve's intuition, which certainly had the failure rate of a below-average bowler, told him something was wrong.

Driving gingerly through downtown, he clenched with each flash of lightning that zigzagged across the sky. The streets were largely empty. Some headlights cut through the falling rain and played tricks on his bad eyes.

He arrived at Don's house a ball of nerves. Streets surrounded the house on three sides. He parked behind the house and sat there, listening to the rain pelt his car. Thunder shook the world and then lightning opened up in the sky almost instantly after. Steve buried his face in his steering wheel.

"Dammit, I can't do this." He felt like such a weakling. He turned the key in the ignition to start the car back up. As he did, he glanced at Don's house. The fence in the backyard was a six-foot privacy fence with lattice windows. It made the yard partly visible. Steve couldn't believe what he saw through them.

"Don?"

Another roll of thunder rumbled through, but Steve was almost too focused on the figure in Don's backyard to notice. He strained his eyes to see through the rain. It had to be Don. Someone was definitely back there, and it almost looked like they were working on something.

But, that would be crazy, he thought to himself.

Steve beeped the horn of his car and waited for Don to turn around. Lightning crashed around him again, preceded by deafening thunder. He put his hand on the horn and left it there. No reaction from Don.

"What the *hell*?"

Now Steve's curiosity overwhelmed his fear. He grabbed his rain jacket and put it on while keeping an eye on Don. Or, the person in Don's backyard. He couldn't imagine why Don wouldn't have turned around when he beeped the horn.

Steve pulled the hood over his head and opened the driver's door. Rain immediately drenched the door and his arm. He lowered his head and jumped from the car. Just as he did, thunder boomed so loudly that he thought it came from inside his head. A bolt of lightning sliced through the oil-black sky and impacted on one of the huge, old trees that surrounded this part of the city.

Steve covered his face and fell back against the open driver's door. When he pulled his hands away, he saw the tree branch falling to the street. Something followed behind it, difficult to discern. It was black, like the sky around it. But it moved like a snake, which made it slightly discernible. It disappeared and he started to turn to get back into his car, but then it reappeared. Swinging toward him. A spark shot out of its end.

Before Steve could think another thought, the power line struck the top of his car and swung around his body. He crumpled to the ground in a burst of light.

ELEVEN

"What do you mean he's dying?"

"The day before you called to tell us you were coming, he was diagnosed with stage four prostate cancer."

"Stage four? How did it get that far?"

"Look at him, Faith. He never says a word."

"Prostate cancer, though. He can fight that off." She cast a teary eye in his direction. "He's strong."

Her mom clinked the sides of her tea cup while she stirred the sugar in. "He's a seventy-nine-year-old man who has been deteriorating for the last five years."

"Mom!"

"When you get to our age, you don't cover reality with jelly."

"What do the doctors say?"

"That he's going to die, Faith. If you aren't here for your dad, why are you here then?" her mother asked, turning the conversation back to what she wanted.

Charity came into the kitchen and clambered onto Faith's lap. Faith's mother stared at her. The wrinkles around her mouth tightened.

"Where's your sister?" Faith inquired.

Charity pointed into the living room. Brooke was dancing circles around her dad's armchair while he smiled.

"Charity, darling, I want you to see something I got for you."

Her mom just wouldn't relent. Charity popped up and went into one of the back rooms with her. Faith felt like she should take a shot of whiskey to deal with the continued onslaught. Her mom returned to the kitchen.

"You were saying?"

"You just disposed of your granddaughter to get the scoop, huh?"

"I'm worried about you, Faith. That's all."

Faith smiled. She felt the history of her mother's lies and vagaries hanging about her neck. To an outsider, they may have seemed like the rueful machinations of a child. However, to the insider such as Faith, there was nothing lighthearted about her mother's insistence.

She decided to feed the beast. It was something weighing on her anyway. "Something is wrong with Don."

Her mother's surprise flowed from cheek to cheek. Faith gave her a response. A substantive response.

"Well…" Her mom fidgeted with the salt shaker, taking the plastic stopper off of the bottom. "What could it be?"

"He has gotten erratic. Impatient. He snapped at the girls a couple of times, and I've never seen him do anything like that."

"He must be stressed, from work. It's a very stressful job he has."

"He's had that same, stressful job for years. I don't think it's any more stressful now than it was in the past. If anything, as he's gotten better at it, it has become a little bit less stressful."

"What could it be then?" One of her mom's cool, blue eyes focused on her from a sideways glance.

"I really don't know."

"You really *do*."

"It would just be speculation."

"That's as good a place to start as any."

"That seems like terrible advice." Her mom didn't flinch. Faith sighed. "I think it's something with the house."

"The house?"

"Yes."

This was almost more than Faith's mom could bear. "I'm still not sure what you mean." But she knew. She just wanted to hear Faith say it.

"Something in the house is changing Don."

Charity ran back into the kitchen. "Grandma, I finished the

puzzle!"

"Already?"

"Yeah." She nudged her way onto her grandma's lap.

Faith and her mom exchanged a look that the conversation would continue later.

* * * * *

Don couldn't believe it was raining this hard. The dry climate hardly ever yielded any precipitation. Making it ever worse was *this* night of all nights. Even as he dug, he couldn't wrap his mind around the reason why he was digging. A *murder*. He had never even lifted a pack of gum from a store. So, to be burying a body was unfathomable.

The thunder rumbled around him. At least it provided cover from his neighbors, who were usually up and about in the late hours. Lightning illuminated the growing hole with frequency. After an hour of digging straight, he stopped and rested his chest on the shovel's handle. His breathing was labored. He never worked out this hard.

Just as he was about to plunge the shovel back into the dirt, a boom almost made him jump into the hole he was digging. Don spun around. His ears rung. He used the shovel to push off and ran toward the back fence. Just a few strides in, there was another boom and a corresponding flash, like a ball of light. His heels dug into the ground as he tried to reverse direction.

It was impossible to tell what had just happened. In the seconds after it did, a moment of clarity emerged from his mind.

People are going to be here soon. Lots of people. He ran to the shed in the backyard and fumbled through the dark for a tarp. There was one folded up on the shelving by the back wall. He grabbed it and headed back into the deluge. *No time to fill the hole back in,* he thought.

Don spread the tarp over the hole. Thankfully, the wind was sedate at that moment. Using dirt as a weight, he spread some over the four corners of the tarp. Lights were coming on in the surrounding homes. The fire station was just a few streets away, so they would be here in minutes.

He looked around frantically, trying to see if there was anything incriminating around. *Other than the grave covered by a tarp,* he thought, there wasn't. He ran into the house via the basement door, fumbled for a light switch, found it and stripped out of all his clothes. He started to put the clothes into the dryer, but then realized that the exhaust vented outside the house. It would be very visible in this weather.

Instead, he put his clothes in the half-bathroom, after using the T-shirt to wipe the water off his body. He ran upstairs and toweled off his hair. There they were, the sirens. Minutes later, as expected, the fire truck's lights illuminated the street behind his house. Don searched through the bathroom for his wife's hair dryer, set it on high, and dried the rest of the moisture out of his hair.

Bending down, he could see through the slit between the curtain and the bathroom window. This was the first time he had taken the time to examine what the hell happened out there. What that boom and ball of light were. He watched as police cars descended on the scene like locusts. Neighbors to the back of his house were out on their porches. They huddled together against the rain, which was tracing the path of the blowing wind again.

Another police car arrived and blocked off the main street past his house. The fire truck moved away from where he had seen the ball of light. Nobody had gotten out of the truck. As he was wondering why, he saw something writhing in the storm. Then, sparks flew into the air, and he saw the electrical cable twist back on itself and slam back into the ground.

An electrical cable. That's all it was. *Thank God,* he thought to himself as he straightened up and headed to his bed. Tucked under the covers, listening to his heartbeat slow down, his mind returned to the task at hand. There was no way he would be able to finish it tonight, he lamented. He couldn't stand another night with that festering body in the house, but it had to be done under the cover of darkness.

Don sighed and rolled over to face the alarm clock. It was one-fifteen in the morning. He set the alarm for two hours, assuming that would be enough time for the electric company to get to the scene and fix the cable. He rolled back over and started to burrow back into a comfortable position. Adrenaline from the moment dropped off a cliff and Don felt a wave of exhaustion tumble through his body.

Just as he was falling asleep, he heard a knock on the front door. He stiffened. Another knock. This one was more demanding. He got up, put a robe on around his T-shirt and shorts and hurried to get to the door. A police officer stood there.

"Sir, I'm sorry to bother you this late, but we are asking all of the neighbors to stay awake for a bit."

Don cleared his throat. "Why's that, officer?"

"There's a power line down behind your house."

"I saw that."

"There's a deceased person next to a car there too."

A lump grew in Don's throat. "Wow, really?"

"Yes, sir. After we get the area secured, we are going to ask residents some questions about the deceased person. If you all know him or her, *et cetera*."

"Okay. Do you know about how long you think it'll take to get that done? It's just that, with work tomorrow…"

The officer scratched his head. "Eh, I'd say it'll take them about an hour, little more, to get that secured."

Don nodded his head and closed the peephole. He turned the porch light off and went back to his bedroom. Through the balcony doors, he could see that an oversized truck with a boom had arrived. The tarp ruffled in a gust of wind but held its position. He sighed and plunged back into bed.

TWELVE

Detective Montoya sat in his unmarked car. The nose of the car was tucked under the yellow crime scene tape blocking the street behind him. The crew from the electric company had shut off power at the local grid to be able to wrangle the power line. He smacked a cigarette out of a fresh pack and lit it with the car lighter.

He eyed the patrolmen who had the unenviable task of standing outside, ready to wave bystanders away. Curious Georges were out on all the stoops of the neighborhood homes. At least this rain would keep them at bay.

Smoke started to fill the car's cabin. He slid the driver's side window down a hair and it vacuumed out. He took another long drag and leaned back into the headrest.

Someone knocked on his window, startling him. He must have briefly fallen asleep. A burnt-out cigarette with a long ash rested in the ashtray. He rolled the window down to its halfway position.

"Detective, they're ready for you," a young officer said.

"Thank you," Montoya responded with a hoarse voice. Between the lack of sleep in the past forty-eight hours and the constant burn of cigarettes, he was surprised his voice functioned at all.

He stepped from the car, and was just about engulfed by the officer who was over six feet tall. In contrast, Montoya couldn't see over a privacy fence on the tips of his toes. The officer was ripped, Montoya was slight. It was a shining example of their police force, past and present. The new officers, often with military backgrounds, were tatted up over bulging muscles. Then the old guard, like Montoya. The donut generation.

Montoya tapped another cigarette out of his pack and lit it while watching the young officer. He could see the officer's face crinkle slightly around his eyes. The new generation didn't like smokers. Montoya smiled and headed to the body.

The rain had slowed to a slight drizzle during his impromptu nap. Still, he pulled the hood of his jacket over his head. Old age only magnified the discomfort of coldness and dampness. He arced around the car and the body lying next to it. A streetlight on the corner behind him hummed and cast a sickly yellow light on the area. Rather than pulling out a flashlight, he decided to take his first look in the scene's natural light.

Montoya reached a point where he was perpendicular to the car, which was parked in the direction of traffic, and the body, which was lying parallel to the car. Squatting down on beleaguered knees, he got a better look at the body. Male. Looked to be thirty-five to forty-five years old. Some charring on the skin, secondary to the electrocution.

The rain had washed away the smell that typically accompanied an electrocution. Montoya had seen dozens of them in his thirty-four years working the homicide unit. He went over to the body and scanned the skin with a small LED flashlight. Deaths like this were just too much for most people. Nights like this were too much. The idea of being a detective lured many. Few were allowed the title, and then of the ones that were, most all burned out. There was no way to have a wife. There was no way to have a family. Even as a single man, he had learned that his own needs and desires always sat backseat to the job. It would be that way, or it would be another job. There was no compromise.

No irregular marks on the body that he could see. Still crouched down, cigarette hanging from his lip, Montoya next searched the surrounding ground for any signs of foul play. Wisps of smoke crept up his nose and eyes, which he expertly kept at bay enough to avoid the discomfort of prolonged exposure.

"Nothing."

"What's that?"

Montoya's shoulders dropped ever so slightly in his crouched and bent-over position. Another part of his job, which he abhorred, was training new detectives. Anyone he had ever cared about in the force had quit or been killed. He had no room in any part of his life for anybody new.

"Nothing, Detective Grud." Montoya called him "Grud" because his actual name, something like Grudowski, was too burdensome. "No signs of foul play."

"So, nothing for us to do here."

Montoya stood up against the groan of his body. They always told him that smoking the cigarettes would do him in, but here he was, sixty-four years old, and everything but the damn cigarettes impacted him.

"Not so fast."

"If there's no foul play, then why'd homicide be involved?"

Another thing Montoya abhorred — a poor speaker. Grud was one of them. "Don't you want to know this guy's story?" Montoya shifted his body to face the young detective.

"If he ain't homicide, then no. It'd probably mean paperwork if I got to know anything about him."

Montoya gestured with his hand in a semicircle around them. "This means nothing to you, does it?"

Grud slowly looked around, his eyebrows dug into the space between his eyes. "What the hell you mean, 'this?' This neighborhood? This guy? What the hell?"

For as much as he couldn't stand trainees, Montoya knew they all hated him just as much. He was so different than the place most of them came from. He was sure he looked like some feeble, ancient mariner of the streets that they expected to find dead at the bottom of the boat any morning. They knew the clock was his enemy and they were just playing out the end of the game.

"This neighborhood abuts the next, which abuts the next, which abuts the next." Montoya enjoyed the hell out of messing with these trainees. "Put it this way, if you had a rotting finger, would you just leave it be?"

"I don't get your shit," Grud answered as he shifted his weight between his feet.

"Let's go talk to some of the neighbors." Grud grunted. "We'll start with this house," Montoya said, pointing to the house on the corner.

"Why that one?"

Montoya pinched the cherry out of the cigarette and put the butt into his back pocket. "You remind me of many women I've been with."

Grud pulled back. "Me? Forget you."

"So many damn questions," Montoya muttered. Raising his voice, he asked, "What house would you start with?"

"For the record…"

"For the record?" Montoya asked with a raised eyebrow. "Who's taking this down?"

"I wouldn't talk to any of the neighbors. This was an accidental death. A freak accident. Who cares what they seen or not?"

"But, *if* you had to choose a house?"

Grud glanced around. "That one," he said, pointing to the house facing the car and dead body.

"Because they could have seen what happened?"

"Exactly."

"Good. Accident or not, Detective, we talk to some people. Never know what you might unearth."

131

Grud stopped talking. Montoya looked at him for another couple of seconds before briskly turning and heading for the house he wanted to see.

They went up a set of stairs from the sidewalk to the house. It had a red front door, guarded by a black security door. Montoya searched for the doorbell. Grud reached around him with one of his gargantuan arms and poked a white button above the mailbox.

Montoya smiled back at him. "Thank you."

A light came on, faintly visible through the rectangular peephole in the door. Montoya took a half-step back. A middle-aged man came to the door and opened the peephole. He looked haggard, worn-out. Dark, half-moons hung under his red eyes. His hair looked like it was running in every direction to get away from his scalp.

Montoya held his badge up. "Detective Roberto Montoya. Can I have a moment of your time?"

The door unlocked. The man fumbled with a set of keys until he cursed and turned on the entryway light. Then he went back to picking through keys before he found the right one and unlocked the security door.

"Come on in."

"This is my partner," Montoya said, gesturing to Grud. He wasn't going to try the name.

The man closed the door and stood with his arms crossed. "So, what can I do for you guys?"

132

* * * * *

Don waited in bed for about an hour and a half before the doorbell rang again. There was no way he could sleep, so he just stared at the ceiling fan that turned on its lowest setting. It emitted a low hum that he had sworn he would try to fix on multiple occasions. He threw on his robe again and headed to the front door.

Don opened the peephole. A detective introduced himself and his partner. The older detective was Montoya.

"Come on in." The detective stepped through the door with some monstrosity following behind him. It was an odd juxtaposition—the aged and wispy-looking detective leading the way for the young, bulky officer. Don noted Detective Montoya's skin, which looked very lived in. The smell of cigarettes was overwhelming. At this moment, Don wished he could have a pack of them.

The officers stood in the middle of the living room, uncomfortably inhabiting the space between the couch and the fireplace. Actually, Detective Montoya looked perfectly at ease, as if this was a family member's house and he was making a routine visit. It was the hulk who looked like he didn't fit. His arms were tightly knit across his chest. His jaw clenched against whatever words Don would throw at them.

"So, what can I do for you guys?" Don purposefully tried to stay simultaneously relaxed and interested. Calm, but on his toes. It took a tremendous effort to stifle the voice echoing in the back of his mind. *You have a dead body upstairs and a hole for it outside.*

"I'm sure you've heard all the commotion behind your house," Detective Montoya started.

"Yeah, hard to miss."

The detective looked around at his surroundings. He glanced up at Don, as if expecting something.

"Sit down! Go ahead." Don took a seat in one of the armchairs next to the fireplace. This was invitation enough for the detectives to sit down.

"So, this man was electrocuted behind your house."

The directness of the statement startled Don. When Detective Montoya didn't say anything else, Don felt compelled to fill the silence. Lest the moment get too weird and raise flags with the detective.

"Are you serious?"

"Very." Again, the silence. This time, Don didn't fill it. "Were you expecting anyone tonight?"

"No, no one," Don answered without hesitation.

"You could come see the body, to be certain, but take a look at this license. It's for a Steve Lischek. Do you recognize that name?"

Don immediately felt his face flush. *Steve*? He thought, "This can't be right."

"What's that?" Detective Montoya inquired as he leaned

134

forward.

Don shook his head. "I know him."

"How?" asked the other detective. Don saw Detective Montoya flash him a nasty look.

"He's a friend of mine."

"A close friend?" Montoya asked, resuming his line of questioning.

"Are you sure that's who's back there?"

Detective Montoya shrugged. "Want to come see him for yourself?"

What in the hell was Steve doing over here? Don thought. He scratched the side of his head for several seconds, slowing down as his thought deepened.

"No, if it's him, I don't want to see."

"You seem pretty confused."

"Well, yeah. Really confused. What was he doing back there? And, he got electrocuted, for real?"

"Electrocuted, for real," Montoya responded. "Looks like it was a freak accident. Power line came down in the storm. Shocked the hell out of him as he was getting out of his car."

"Can't believe it." Don spun Steve's license in his fingers, as if he was trying to feel each molecule in it to make sure it was real.

"How long have you lived here, Mr . . . actually, I just realized that I haven't even taken down your name yet."

"Don." He came to his senses and realized the detective likely wanted more than just his first name. "Don Paxton."

"Mr. Paxton, how long have you lived here?"

"About seven months. Eight."

"This is a house with plenty of history."

Don stopped reflecting on the license and looked up at Detective Montoya. "What do you mean, history?"

"How about this?" Detective Montoya asked while standing up. "Take my card," he said, handing it to Don. "It's late. Call me tomorrow and we'll meet up for a coffee. I'll tell you more about the house, and you can tell me more about Mr. Lischek, okay?"

Don nodded, even though he was a bit perturbed to be teased like that. The detective moved to the front door and paused there.

"You know, I think you may have a leak in one of your plumbing or sewer lines." He looked Don directly in the eyes. "It smells kind of funky in here. Dangerous to have gases like that floating around."

This caused a lump to swell up in Don's throat. "Yeah, we've been in the middle of several projects."

Detective Montoya held a finger up, "Dangerous gases." He

opened the door and stepped out. Don immediately heard the snap of a lighter and could see the glow of the cigarette's cherry through the peephole.

He stepped back from the front door and watched the two detectives move down the sidewalk and out of sight. A contained gasp of air finally released. Don couldn't come to grips with the fact that Steve had been electrocuted to death. Behind his house, no less.

Lest you forget, Don, there's still the issue of the body, he thought. The voice in his head had an edge that made it seem like it was someone else's.

He ran up the stairs to his bedroom and looked out of the French doors to the second-story deck and backyard. All of the spinning lights, whether police or utility company, were gone. Standing there in the dark for a couple of minutes, he saw no movement. The storm's fury had tapered off. All he could make out by looking at the puddles on the ground was a light drizzle.

Don searched for and found a new digging outfit, comprised of another pair of old painting jeans, double layer of socks, and multiple layers of T-shirt, long-sleeve shirt, and weatherproof jacket. The clock said 2:45 a.m. That left him enough time to finish the digging. He put a hat on and donned his gloves as he went into the backyard. Pulling the tarp off of the hole, he was dismayed to see it filled with several inches of water. The next several hours were going to be unbearable.

* * * * *

"So, what did you think about him?"

Montoya studied Grud's face before answering. "I thought nothing. What do you mean?"

"I mean, he seemed kind of nervous. Didn't you get that vibe?"

"No. Have a good night, detective," Montoya lied as he got into his car, using the open car door as a brace. He drove off under street lamps and through the empty streets of the city. His house was located in the northeast part of the city. When he had purchased the house some forty years ago, it was a decent area. The home was a small bungalow constructed in 1948. Unfortunately, because of gentrification and the general rise in property values of homes in many other parts of the city, these types of homes had become a last resort for low-income people. That left him clinging to a neighborhood rapidly deteriorating around him.

Still, he didn't let the condition of his neighbors' homes alter how he cared for his own. His was the only one with outdoor lights lining the path to the front door. Manicured bushes, planted years ago and now grown to a height that provided the privacy of a fence, stood guard along his property line. Maintaining this yard was therapeutic for Montoya. It was usually how he spent the first part of his Saturday mornings. Sunday was reserved for watching sports, another type of therapy for his haunted mind.

Montoya pulled the Crown Victoria up the driveway. It chugged as he turned it off. Old thing needed a trip to the department's mechanic. In spite of the department's urging to turn the car in, he clung to it. Probably too long. His neighbor's light was on. Low thuds were audible. He and the neighbor had reached an agreement. Fridays and Saturdays were the neighbor's to go ape-shit. Party, girls, booze, whatever. The rest of the days, things had to be contained. Montoya had a bad disease of barely being able to sleep, and without this agreement he'd never get any.

He squeezed his key into the front door lock and shoved the door open with his left shoulder. Beeping immediately started, and he headed to the kitchen to punch his code into the alarm. He returned to the front door, latched it shut, removed his jacket and fell into the recliner sitting in the middle of his living room. *No TV tonight*, he thought. *Just need to get to sleep.*

Montoya leaned over the right armrest of the chair and pulled out a small tin box. He opened it and the pungent aroma of its contents burst out. The chair seemed to sink in lower as he took a drag from a half-smoked joint. Smoke slowly slipped from between his lips. He held the joint out in front of his face and analyzed it. Amazing how that little thing was defending him against all the pain. The weed was another part of the deal he had with the neighbor.

Montoya pulled the handle up on the recliner, leaned back, and prayed to whatever God would listen to let him fall asleep tonight.

* * * * *

Faith sat in the backyard with her parents and the girls. The girls were playing hide-and-go-seek through the garage, side yard and into the house. Every now and again, Faith could hear one of them scream. At other times she would hear them bicker about rules, who had broken them, and new rules to take care of possible rule-breaking.

Faith could feel her mother staring at her out of the corner of her eye. Without looking, she said, "Yes, Mother?"

"Our conversation is far from over," she whispered.

"I don't know what else you want me to say. I told you what I thought was going on."

Charity ran out of the garage shrieking. She flew past both of them, with Brooke in hot pursuit. Of the two, perhaps surprisingly, Charity was more athletic.

"You know what I want you to say." After Faith didn't respond, her mom sighed. "I want you to say that you are going to use those powers to figure out what's going on at your house."

Faith bolted up from her chair. "Mom, you're almost as delirious as Dad! You've been sitting here letting all this nonsense fill your mind for too long. Powers? What on Earth are you talking about? I only believe in one power…"

"Oh, here we go." Her mom put her head in her hand.

"Well, you know how I feel. How could there be spirits in my house when I believe in God?"

"Could be God's spirits."

"I don't believe that. And, I don't believe that I've got any extra powers that others don't." Faith grabbed the hair hanging on both sides of her head and forced it back into a ponytail.

"Oh, dear…" her mother started, and the words chased Faith back into the house.

140

"Enough, Mom." Faith headed back for her dad who was still by the radio. She looked at her watch and heard her mother trudge into the house. Five hours into the stay and she wondered how much more of this she'd be able to take.

THIRTEEN

Montoya tapped the plastic cup with his fingers, listening to the dull thud that they produced. This guy, this Paxton, was already ten minutes late. Montoya hoped for his sake that this wasn't a blowoff. Particularly since Paxton was the one that chose this place. Starbucks. Montoya was pretty sure the "ugh" he felt inside reflected on his face. With all the coffee shops in this town, all the places that could have been unique as a setting, Paxton had to pick this brightly staffed, clean location.

"Oh, well," he said out loud, commenting on his ruminations.

One of the two doors into the Starbucks opened and a teenager came in. Black eyeliner, black baggy jeans. Spiked hair and piercings on his face. *What agony is that kid in?* Montoya asked himself.

"Detective Montoya?"

The voice startled him. He pivoted in his chair and found himself looking up directly at Don Paxton.

"Oh, hello, Mr. Paxton," he said, standing up and extending his hand. Paxton took his hand with a firm and very brief grip.

Montoya studied the man better in the day's light. He was late-thirties to early-forties. He had dark, thinning hair. Not so thin that it forced a comb-over or a shave, but in half a decade it would be all gone. Today, Paxton wore a suit. It looked nice, expensive. He certainly looked like a lawyer, down to the haggard face hiding sharp and cunning eyes.

"Mr. Paxton, did you have an all right night after we disturbed you?"

"I did. You?"

Montoya smiled. "At my age, restful nights become more elusive by the day. That's why I drink this," he said, holding up a coffee cup. "Endlessly." Montoya gestured over to the line.

"No, thank you. I don't drink it."

"Really? I've never managed without it."

Now, Don smiled. "Sometimes, I'm not sure how I do."

They sat for a few moments in a pregnant silence. Don broke it. "So, what are we doing, Detective?"

"You wanted to know about your house, right? I thought?"

"Sure, but I didn't gather that telling me about my house was all *you* wanted."

"No," Montoya said while turning the cup on the table, "it wasn't." He looked up. "A little *quid pro quo* never hurt, right?"

"Depends."

"That's a lawyer answer, isn't it?" Montoya said with a smirk that disappeared as quickly as it had flashed across his face.

"Okay, Steve Lischek," Don started. "We met in law school. I moved here just for law school, so I didn't know anyone. Steve was my first friend."

143

"Both lawyers, huh?"

"Yeah, but Steve practiced patent litigation. Pretty high-end stuff."

"What's your practice?"

"I thought this was about Steve."

Montoya pursed his lips. "Just small talk, Mr. Paxton. Just small talk."

Paxton leaned back in his chair. "I'm a commercial litigator. Contract cases mainly."

"High-end stuff too?"

"Fairly. Not as specialized as Steve, though. Anyway, getting back to Steve, he's always been pretty much the same. High energy, high spender. High ego, certainly an ego on that guy."

"You know," Montoya started, leaning over the small, aluminum table, "I'm not one to talk much about marriage, having been divorced twice. But, that guy couldn't have fit well into the husband-wife-best-friend tripartite."

"Never said he was my best friend. He was my first friend here. You're right, though, he wouldn't have fit into that relationship at all. Honestly, he didn't even try. Once I met Faith, there was just an unspoken understanding that it was over. Nothing negative, but just nothing to go forward on."

"The bachelor as the third wheel doesn't work."

"That's right."

"So, you're married?"

"Yes."

"How long?"

Paxton smiled, a reminder that the conversation was straying from the intended topic. "Eleven years."

"Children?" Montoya asked meekly. "Come on, you've got me at a Starbucks at ten in the morning. This is just chit-chat."

"For the record, *you've* got me here. I have two daughters, twins."

"Twins! Wow, I couldn't imagine that. One at a time was enough."

Paxton obliged Montoya in the small talk. "You? Kids?"

Montoya felt his mood darken slightly. "Yes, three. Two from the first marriage. One from the second." He took a sip of his coffee. "Back to Mr. Lischek. Was he currently in a relationship, if you know?"

"Not that I know of. Steve, well, he was overly aggressive with women because he was insecure. At least, that's what I think. What he wanted most he pushed away with how he acted."

"Did you all see each other that often?"

"Like I said before, not that much anymore."

An employee came up to their table and asked if everything was okay. Montoya nodded and she went away.
"When was the last time you had seen him?"

He watched as Don hesitated. "Been a while. Probably, six to nine months."

Montoya was well-trained in the art of human deception. He noticed something in Paxton, or at least his subconscious noted something that triggered his intuition. Intuition was a tool Montoya had learned to trust without question, without doubt, over the course of his career. Years on the street, years dealing with every machination man could throw at him had sharpened that tool into the leading point of an arrow. Which is why the next question was a follow-up.

"Oh yeah? What for?" Now, Montoya studied Paxton as he responded.

"Think it was just some function for work."

Montoya took out a small pad of paper tucked into a leather flip billfold that he carried everywhere. "Good. That must have been on your calendar, right?"

Paxton's face contorted. "Hey, what's this about? I thought you just wanted some more information on Steve, and now you're treating me like I'm a suspect?"

Montoya closed the billfold. The bluff had its desired impact.

"Just covering all of my bases, Mr. Paxton. I don't think you had anything to do with your friend's death. That was clearly a freak accident."

"What are you doing then?"

"There's one thing that I can't figure out. Why was Mr. Lischek behind your house, late at night and in one of the worst thunderstorms we've had in years?"

Paxton shrugged his shoulders. "Beats me. I hadn't talked to him. We had no plans."

Montoya decided to employ another of his interrogation techniques, which was to abruptly change the line of questioning midstream.

"Your wife and kids, where were they last night?"

"Excuse me?"

When a person was so focused on one topic, the change to another often revealed truth. Unless the person was coached. Montoya used this technique on an almost daily basis.

"Your family, I didn't see or hear anything from them when I was in your house last night."

"Look," Paxton said as he stood up, "I don't know what you're after, but I'm done here."

Montoya stood up too. "Don't you want to hear about your house?"

Paxton waved him off. "No, not from you," he said as he

walked off.

Montoya watched him walk away and said, "I think you do."

* * * * *

Don slammed his car door shut and sat brooding for several seconds. *What the hell was with that detective?* he thought. *How could he have any idea?* And, yet, Don had the sick feeling that the detective had read him like an open book. At a minimum, Don knew that his performance in the Starbucks had only cracked the door open more than it was before.

A thought skipped across his mind, like a flat stone hitting the surface of the water a few times before sinking into darkness. *Kill Montoya.*

"What?" he asked, trying to brush the thought away. He started the car but just as he did, a sharp jolt shot through his head.

"Damn!" he groaned. He gripped the steering wheel with both hands, fighting off a tidal wave of nausea that hit him after the pain. With several breaths, the pain lessened. Don put the car in reverse, relieved it was over but confused as to what that was. As he sat waiting for traffic to pass, the pain rocked him again.

"Ah!!" This time, he put his head on the steering wheel. He tried to control the nausea but it was too late. Vomit shot out like it was from a body he didn't control. "Ugh..." Someone rapped on his window. He tilted his head slowly. It was Detective Montoya.

The detective said something unintelligible through the

driver's side window. Don managed to raise his hand and push the button to lower the window.

"Mr. Paxton, are you okay?" He saw Montoya lean toward the car. "Is that vomit?" Don nodded. "Okay, let me call you an ambulance."

"No, no," Don said, shaking his head while resting it on the side of the steering wheel. "I . . . I just got sick."

"I see that."

"I just need to go home and rest." He wiped his mouth with the back of his forearm.

"You sure you don't want me to call the paramedics?"

Don sat back and stretched his neck. "Yes," he said with a beleaguered smile. "Thank you, but I think I'll just go rest. Probably just everything that's been going on. Steve and everything."

Montoya looked at him, and Don looked away to try to hide the vague remnants of the thought that had just crossed his mind.

* * * * *

Don choked back vomit for most of the drive home. It was a stone's throw from his house, but on two occasions he was forced to pull over. During the interludes between the sickness, he tried to recall what he had eaten that would cause this. Nothing came to mind. He had all the symptoms of food poisoning.

Don got to the house and twisted his hands on the steering

wheel while the garage door opened. He barely made it to the bathroom before projectile vomiting into the toilet. Gasping for air, he ripped some toilet paper off the roll and wiped his mouth. Then he rested against the bathroom wall, one arm still wrapped around the toilet.

Wish Faith was here, he thought. She'd take care of him. Instead, he was alone and wretched again into the toilet. It was a dry heave this time, painful. He sighed and fell back against the wall. After a few minutes of staring at the toilet and monitoring signs of any more vomiting spells, Don slowly got on a knee and wiped the toilet seat clean. He dabbed his face with a damp hand towel and headed upstairs to the bedroom. Exhaustion overcame him and he fell asleep while pushing one shoe off with his other foot.

As far as he could tell, he was instantly in a dream. It startled him because he rarely remembered dreams. It was even stranger for him to be so lucid in the middle of one. He felt a surge of panic and tried to open his eyes, or at least he imagined this was what he was trying to do.

Nothing happened though, and the dreamworld took a clearer form around him.

Everything started to fit into its right place. The dining room table. The sofa in the living room. Two colors pixelated in the scene: red and green. Then the room trembled. It drifted off, shook harder, and then came back into focus. But, this wasn't their house. The floors were a different color. He tried to take a step and it was like he was trapped in gel. The floor was carpet. The walls were gray. Everything was gray. A strange lullaby, like someone playing three keys on a piano, came from upstairs.

Don tried to shout, but a foreign, distorted sound came from his mouth. An alien language. He felt the panic again, but then the lullaby got louder and he was immediately compelled to discover its source. He tried to move again, and met the same effect. He *thought* about moving and it happened. Thought about going to the stairs and he was there. Thought about going up the stairs and his body . . . Don looked down. There was no body. He tried to touch himself but his hands wouldn't move. He thought about touching himself and got confused, then started to lose the focus of the space he was in.

The lullaby grew in volume. It brought Don back into the room, and it came from the room. He glided up the stairs on pure energy of thought. He reached the door to the room and tried to open it with his hand. When that didn't work, he thought again about the door being open and it was. The room was dark, almost as if light knew it would be sucked into another dimension if it tried to enter. A crib perched next to the only window in the room. There was an odd clarity around the crib, like it was static, two dimensional and drawn against the black walls of the room. Like the burnt-in image on the backs of eyelids. The lullaby came from a mobile hanging above the crib.

He floated over and stood over it. A baby boy was asleep, swaddled in a blanket. Don stood there, a peace coming over him that he hadn't felt since moving into the house. He mouthed, "There, there," and leaned closer to the baby. He imagined his hand resting on the baby's head. Imagined the hand rubbing the baby's head. The baby started to stir, and he tried to withdraw his hand. It wouldn't move. The baby's eyes snapped open. There were no pupils, just black orbs suspended in a chalky, white body. In an instant, an adult's face replaced the baby's and flew up at him.

Don shot up from the bed, yelling out and swinging around his body. Orienting himself, his hand came to rest on a framed picture of the girls placed on the nightstand next to him. Still mired in the fright of the dream, he put the picture on his chest and fell back into a fitful sleep.

F O U R T E E N

Montoya woke up to a dull, overcast day. It was rare for him to have slept this long. Rarer still for there to be cloud cover at this time of the morning. He stretched, and what stretch meant for a man of his age was hands at his sides, a shudder through his body, and then wishing he could oil his joints to get them moving.

He shuffled to the kitchen to start a pot of coffee. The house groaned around him as it woke up too. They were in tandem, and had been for decades. Montoya collected the paper from his front porch and briefly looked around the neighborhood. Nothing stirred. He could hear traffic from the big street just two blocks over.

The patio door slammed shut behind him, reminding him that he needed to replace the pneumatic closer. It wasn't often he let a repair linger that long. The newspaper unfolded with the weight of its contained events and Montoya sat down to a cup of black coffee. There was no breakfast for him anymore. His body didn't burn enough calories to warrant a meal at this time of day.

That guy — Don Paxton — came to his mind as he had all night. Not in dreams, Montoya didn't have them. Paxton came to him in startled fits just when he was about to fall asleep. Like an alarm that kept sounding, keeping Montoya from slumber that he would not dare call restful. This type of lingering over a situation had only occurred a few times in Montoya's career. All the other times involved incidents that Montoya tried to forget. The Hassidy multiple murder. The Chen shooting in a pizza restaurant. He had been on both those cases. In fact, he had just started investigations into those two men when the catastrophes

153

occurred.

They were such different circumstances, he thought to soothe himself. Both Hassidy and Chen had a history of mental illness. Montoya found nothing of the sort in Paxton. In fact, Paxton for all intents and purposes, seemed tremendously normal. A good job, nice house, presumably good family. *Except for that evasion when asked about them.*

He stepped out of the shower, steeped in thoughts, and mechanically removed what could be called his uniform from the closet. It wasn't issued by the police department. It was just something that he wore every day to work. Pressed khaki pants, blue dress shirt with a white undershirt. He topped it off with a gray windbreaker as he walked out to the garage.

He took a detour, though. His study was the room next to his bedroom, and quite honestly, the place he spent the most time. In descending order of time spent, it went study, living room, bedroom. Probably kitchen before bedroom. The bedroom, to Montoya, was a last resort. The study was long with a big floor-to-ceiling window. It was an old leaded window, so it was broken up with a honeycomb of squares. Similarly sized bookshelves lined the room, and were brimming over with books of all types. Fiction, nonfiction, old, new, collectible, paperback. Montoya went to his desk and pulled out an accordion folder. He searched for the documents related to Hassidy and Chen, pulled them out and then headed to his car. It would be useful reading material for the stakeout.

The brisk morning air found ways through the old walls of his garage. It jolted his senses to pass from the house to the chilly interior of his vehicle. He pushed a button on his garage door opener and waited, tapping his finger to some silent melody.

154

Montoya pushed a tape into his car stereo and the last twenty seconds of *Hung on You* came on. He coaxed a cigarette out of a pack that crinkled in his hand, then touched the head of a tiny, golden baby taped to the top of his dashboard.

"Que Dios me bendiga," he whispered as he made the sign of the cross on himself.

He backed the car out and could hear the gravel crush through the slightly open window that sucked out a stream of cigarette smoke. His big idea for the day was to go to Paxton's house and just monitor. It was 70 percent of his job, the monitoring. Most of the rest was paperwork. Just a small fraction of his time actually involved anything exciting. And, exciting to an outside person was not exciting to him anymore, just frightening. It's why he had rookies around.

Montoya reached Paxton's house in just under ten minutes. They were nearly neighbors. He parked between an old Chevy Blazer and an even older Ford F-150. He shut the car off and organized the Hassidy file on the center console next to him. The center console was one of the few privileges he had taken with the department's mechanics. They custom-built him a reading tray that could be pulled out, much like those found on airplanes. Montoya didn't have much of the new technology his counterparts did. But, he spent hours upon hours in his car, and figured that this request wasn't too extravagant. One of his other additions to the car was a lumbar support for his seat. That was his own purchase, though.

The Hassidy file was very thick. It had been a yearlong investigation of his before the ultimate multiple murder at the Hassidy residence. Several incidents at the house preceded his involvement. Two domestic disturbance calls. A time when

Hassidy's parents called the police and asked them to take their son away. Thom Hassidy was twenty-three years old when he killed his entire family.

Montoya got involved after the call from Thom's family. He took the kid to breakfast, as was his modus operandi. Montoya was often tasked with the juveniles. Everyone in the department knew he had a different level of tolerance for them than anyone else. He was often their last chance before they'd be sent away to juvenile detention or the state mental health facility.

It was a bright morning when they met. Not that Montoya necessarily attributed any positive aspect to a bright morning. Oftentimes, the youths he met with were so deeply enshrouded in their own blackness that they wouldn't be able to tell you what any part of the world around them looked like. Montoya understood that blackness, that grief, sense of loss and longing. He went through it when he lost Margaret and his own children. When the kids came to him and he saw the blackness in them, he knew. And, they knew. Grief operates in a universal language.

That's what he saw in Hassidy. A glazed look. Watery eyes. Pale complexion. Hassidy was a good-looking boy. Over six feet tall. Appeared to be athletic or at least have the structure to be it. This was a young man who should have been outside playing sports, sporting a glowing tan and teenage girls on his arms. They sat across from each other for a long time, almost thirty minutes. Montoya knew that the worst thing to do with these kids, with anyone suffering from the blackness, was to jump right in.

"I've got as long as you need," Montoya said after he finished nearly all of his coffee.

Hassidy glanced up at him. There was something in the look,

156

in the eyes, that Montoya caught. It was something that he would later regret missing. But, the boy started talking before he could put more focus on it. "I need a long time."

"I know where you are. That can't be force…"

The boy flashed a smile as sharp and dark as an obsidian blade. "You don't know where I'm at. You've never been where I'm at."

Montoya turned the coffee cup around in his fingers. He marveled at the naiveté of youth. Of how blinded the young were by their delusions of grandeur. Most of his colleagues would have responded and told this young man, this young boy, that he was an idiot and didn't know anything. Most adults would take that approach. Part of Montoya's finesse in this situation was anticipating the teenage hubris and letting it wash off his shoulders.

"I probably haven't been where you're at. That part's right. Probably not a lot of people that have. Everyone's perspective is different. But I've been to some places. Maybe similar ones. Wherever you travel, when it's a bad road, you end up in the same place. I've been to that place." Montoya set his face solidly and watched Hassidy.

"What is this, by the way?"

"This?" Montoya asked with a sigh. "This is your last chance, Thom. The places you go from here only get worse."

Hassidy seemed to contemplate this, as if wondering if it were a promise. "Juvenile detention."

157

"State mental rehabilitation institution. Probably worse there. I'd rather be around a bunch of predators than a bunch of wounded animals."

Thom chuckled. There was something in his demeanor that threw Montoya off. There was the darkness, the depression. There was an almost equally powerful sense of confidence. Typically, the two didn't intermingle.

"It was my dad's connections that got me this last chance, huh?"

"That's where the initial call came from. I do this for anyone that asks, though. Sometimes, I even do it for people that don't ask."

"So, what am I asking for?"

"You tell me."

Montoya fast-forwarded in his mind and then snapped out of the recollection. He jumped to the center of the car when someone rapped on his window.

"Oh, Christ," he muttered. It was Paxton.

"Seems like an interesting place to be taking in the morning."

Montoya had nothing to say. He just started the car and drove off.

* * * * *

Don lazily dragged a trash can to the back fence. He followed up with another. The frosted grass cracked under his feet. His intermittent breaths attacked the cold air around him before succumbing and dissipating. The gate to the street behind their house was locked from the outside, so the next step was to make his way inside and then around to the back. He followed this weekly ritual in a haze. Caught up in thoughts about his family. Desperately missing Faith. After an unproductive telephone call the night before, he felt the internal pressure of despair and loneliness.

His skin objected to the blast of warm air inside the house and then the subsequent return to cold air. Turning the corner to the back of the house, he saw an unfamiliar car parked there. It was white, looked like it should have been in a seventies' cop movie. He went to open the gate, keeping his eye on the car. After he pulled the trash cans out, he stood there and realized who was sitting in the car.

"What the hell?"

Don strode over to the car. He rapped his knuckles on the window. Detective Montoya jumped as if he was asleep. Montoya faintly heard Don say something, they looked at each other for another moment and then the detective calmly started the car and drove away. He did it as if nothing was out of the ordinary. Don watched the car turn the corner and head away from his house. Something snapped inside his mind and he ran for his house. He slammed his shoulder into the front door when he didn't get the latch opened fast enough. Keys, shoes and he was down in the garage, waiting for the door to open. He sped back and down the short driveway, disregarding the possibility of oncoming traffic. Surprisingly, about half a mile down the road he could still see the detective's car.

Was it a dare? Or, did the detective think that he wouldn't come after him?

He forced the car into drive and the cold tires slipped on the cold pavement. They caught and both he and the car shot forward. At eighty miles per hour, Don caught up to the detective's car in no time. He pulled alongside the car, in the lane for oncoming traffic.

"Pull the fuck over!" he yelled through the passenger window. Detective Montoya shot him an angry look and then threw his overhead lights on. There were several seconds where they drove in parallel, neither knowing who was going to slow down and pull over. Finally, Detective Montoya slowed his car to a stop and Don stopped in front of him.

He jumped from the car and ran back to the detective's car. "What's your problem?! You're staking out behind my house now?"

"Mr. Paxton, go back to your vehicle." He saw the detective put his hand on his hip.

"Oh, you're gonna *shoot* me now? First thing on a Tuesday morning for you? Shoot someone that you're harassing?" A car beeped its horn. Don was standing in the middle of the street.

"Get back to your vehicle, Mr. Paxton. Don't make this worse than it is."

Don could see the old man's body trembling. He didn't know if it was the cold or the adrenaline or both. He didn't care either. It just made him snicker. There was a rage in him that he felt like he couldn't control, like he didn't want to. He kicked the front fender of the detective's car and walked back to his own. The trunk of his car seemed like a good place to stop.

Detective Montoya caught up after checking the passing traffic. "You've lost your mind, Mr. Paxton."

"Damn right I have. I've got a cop harassing me."

"This isn't harassment. You've opened the door to a whole lot more scrutiny with these actions, though."

Don waved him off. "You think I care?"

"If you don't care, then why did you chase after me?"

A gust of wind shot down the corridor of homes surrounding them. It seemed to lower Don's fuming temper. "It pissed me off."

"That I was behind your house?"

"That you were staking out my house!"

He saw Detective Montoya check the traffic again. "Mad enough to chase down a police officer and violate enough rules of the road to be put in jail?"

"Guess so."

"Look, Mr. Paxton." The detective shoved his hands into his coat. "I'll offer you one of two things. You choose. First, I call a couple of my buddies and they take you downtown and charge you. Book you. You'll get to spend at least a few hours in jail."

"Enticing. Can't wait to hear what the other choice is."

"You come with me. We get breakfast, and I tell you about what happened in that house of yours."

Don couldn't contain his confusion. "My house? You're still on that?"

The detective fixed a look on him. "Still on that."

"I've got to work."

"You're out here in your pajamas. Doesn't seem so imperative." The detective removed a cigarette and lit it.

"Thirty minutes."

"Mick's Diner. Three blocks east from here."

"Seriously? That's a scummy place."

Worn creases around the detective's mouth deepened. "Don't get your white collar feathers ruffled. See you there."

In all honesty, just about every place around Don's house was scummy. They lived two blocks from the busiest and longest street in the city. It was a mad chemist's experiment. Black people. White people. Asians. Indians. Every color imaginable. Ninety percent of them were the dregs, holed up in hourly motels. Wandering the street with liquor bottles wrapped in brown paper bags. Standing in the middle of the street, tripping out on passing cars. Prostitutes, drug dealers, pimps, meth heads. It was a diluted Skid Row. So Don felt a little bit sheepish when he pulled his model year BMW into Mick's Diner.

Technically, it was "ick's iner." The "M" and the "D" were long burnt out. On his way into the diner, a black man in tattered clothes asked him for money and a white woman tipped a hip in his direction while she leaned on the exterior of the building. It was 7:58 a.m.

He saw Detective Montoya already seated in a teal-colored booth. That was something else about Mick's. It was stuck in 1950s decor, but not in a nostalgic way. It looked like it had been built then, deteriorated since then, and that's about it.

"Don't order the eggs."

Don sighed. "Why not?"

"Can't vouch for them." Detective Montoya lit up a cigarette.

"How long you been doing that?"

"Doing what?" the detective asked without looking up from the menu. A menu that he likely knew by heart and needed to study less than the back of his hands.

"Smoking."

"Since I was eleven."

"Wow! And, they say it's bad for you."

"It is," he answered through a billow of smoke.

"Isn't there a ban on smoking indoors?"

"Let's get to the point, Mr. Paxton." Don pulled his shoulders back. "That house you moved into, it's no good."

"Seems pretty solidly built to me."

"When I saw it was in foreclosure, I hoped it would just stay that way forever."

"That's a strange thing to say about a house."

"That house . . . has had many strange things happen in it."

"Okay, so how about you stop being so cryptic and tell me what you're talking about."

Don watched as the detective brought his cup of coffee up to his lips slowly. "It was 1961," he said over the brim. "A family called the Sturlings lived in your house. The husband was a local businessman. Advertising. The wife was stay-at-home. They had a child named Philip."

Don felt the hair on the back of his neck stand up at the mention of the boy's name.

"Everything was copacetic in the family for several years. Then, according to neighbors, things started to deteriorate."

"Wait, were you on this case?"

"Yes."

Don chuckled. "Not to be rude, but doesn't that make you old as dirt to be active on the police force."

"It makes me old as dirt for anything."

"Don't they have some mandatory retirement age?"

"Not our jurisdiction." The detective stirred his coffee and picked at the hash browns the waitress had placed in front of him. "Back to the story?"

"Yeah, right."

"Things started to deteriorate. There were fights. Neighbors heard screaming. Understand, that was a time and generation of the deaf ear. Especially so when it came to domestic issues. Neighbors saw Mrs. Sturling looking physically harmed on a couple of occasions. Again, they reported nothing."

Don squirmed in his seat. It was like something was starting to heat the area under him.

"Everything culminated on February 12, 1961. Mr. Sturling killed his wife via blunt force trauma to her head. They found a room up in the attic. It had all sorts of instruments for torture. I remember going into that room. Only once."

"Why?"

Detective Montoya shook his head. "I can't describe it for you. You haven't felt it up there?"

"In the attic? No, it feels normal up there to me," Don said. Detective Montoya scrutinized him. "Feels just like an attic."

"We found several bodies buried in the backyard," Montoya said.

165

"The son, Philip," Don responded. Detective Montoya looked confused. "Philip. Didn't the husband kill him too? A neighbor told us so."

"No, none of those bodies were Philip's. Philip, last I checked, is still alive."

FIFTEEN

Faith packed their bags into the car while the girls played on the front lawn. It was a beautiful winter morning. Chilly but not freezing. Surprisingly, the sun was shining in a clear sky. This time of year in Ohio didn't see many instances like this. Faith took it as a good omen that they were headed home. Truth be told, she didn't need any omen to be on her way. Three weeks with her mom was enough.

"Girls, go say one last goodbye to your grandparents," she shouted out through the interior of the car. They screeched and went back inside the house. She stuffed the girls' small suitcases, almost novelty suitcases, into the trunk. She grabbed one of their backpacks and the contents spilled when she accidentally picked it up by the bottom of a strap.

"Dang it!" She sighed and bent down to scoop the jumbled mess into the backpack. That's when she noticed something that she thought she'd never see again. It was the doll they had found at the house. Wrapped in a blanket, with an ill-fitting dress on. It looked entirely wrong. Like putting a pretty sundress on a vagrant.

Something cold gripped her as she held the doll. Her breath suddenly became visible on the next exhale. She disconnected from reality, not voluntarily. She was taken somewhere. A place that was dark, dimly lit by outside light. There was a gleaming steel table in the room. Strange things hung from the side of it. She started to head over to the table.

"Mama?"

167

Faith fell back onto her rear.

"Mama, mama?" one of her daughters called out.

"Faith?"

The voices were like a synthesized layer playing on a loop deep in her mind. She consciously thought about blinking and was finally able to. The blink helped her retrieve her senses. She looked around her and saw the concerned faces. The scared face of Charity. Her dad's face, just above the window sill.

She looked down at the doll in her hand and used it to restore her control to the moment. "Brooke Margaret Paxton, where in the *hell* did you get this?"

Brooke tried to snatch it out of her hand, but she pulled back in time. The two stared at one another, a menacing stare, until Faith's mom picked Brooke up.

"Brooke, answer your mother."

Faith shook her head and got back to her feet. "No need. I know where it's from, and it's gone for good."

"No, Mama! Don't hurt my doll!"

"It's gone!" Faith screamed out as she walked back into the house. She stormed into the kitchen and threw the doll in the trash under the sink. Brooke was crying outside. Charity had taken a seat in the car, trying to avoid the confrontation.

Returning outside with the ferocity of a soldier's step she snapped at Brooke, "Now, get in the car," Brooke complied silently.

"Darling," her mom started.

"It's okay, Mom," Faith said, trying to brush her off.

"Darling, did you see something again?" she whispered.

Faith directed a cross look at her mom. "No, mother, I didn't see anything. Like I told you, I don't see anything." She gave her a terse hug and then got into the car.

*****

It was Don's turn to demonstrate his unbridled surprise.

"Mr. Paxton, are you all right?" The words registered, and Don nodded his head. "What is it?" the detective continued.

Don's mind immediately focused on concealing what he was thinking. Was there any harm in telling the detective? Telling him that his daughters had seen Philip. Not telling him the rest? Don ultimately decided against it. Anything he told Detective Montoya would just further spur the interest already generated.

"No, nothing. Just startled to hear about something like this happening in our house."

"You didn't seem startled until I told you that the son was still alive," Detective Montoya answered quickly, voicing the follow-up question that Don wished he hadn't.

"I can't really explain my reaction right now. I'm shocked. I'm still reeling from my friend getting electrocuted behind my house. Can't you understand that?" was all Don mustered. He knew it was extraordinarily weak.

Detective Montoya leaned back, keeping his penetrating eyes concentrated on Don. That started to become overwhelming. Don felt the heat rise not just from his seat now, but from all around his body. It was as if an alarm was going off, but he couldn't tell if it was from inside himself or not.

"You know, I was on two very significant cases in my career," the detective said after taking his time to chew a mouthful of food. "They were just two years apart, and I hadn't really reflected on them to gain the knowledge that I have today."

Don took a sip of his water hoping that it would cool his nerves. It tasted like the inside of a pipe. He cursed himself for coming to this shit-hole restaurant, for allowing himself to get involved in this conversation with this man. It was a trap. A trap laid by a tremendously skilled hunter.

"I've probably got to get going," Don muttered.

"No, not yet," Detective Montoya said with an urgency that permeated his old hands such that they trembled. "Just hear me out for a few more minutes."

"Just hurry."

"These cases, the point is that many years later I was able to piece together commonalities between the two men that committed the crimes." There was a pause before he added the next part. "These two men that killed their families."

This shook Don. "Killed their families? What's that have to do

170

with me?"

"I want you to know you can speak to me."

"About what exactly? *Killing my family*?"

"Just if you are having any strange feelings or thoughts."

Don shoved up from the table. "I don't know what the *hell* your problem is, but I'm getting a lawyer, okay? This is harassment. Killing my *family*?"

He made for the exit of the restaurant, but heard Detective Montoya call out one more thing before he got through it. "Mr. Paxton, where is your family right now?"

* * * * *

Montoya knew he said too much even as the air crossed his vocal cords. He knew it when the thought manifested in his mind. All the years of training. All the patience in the world. Yet, he was human, and he made a human mistake. With Paxton on the edge, possibly considering trusting in him, he pushed too hard. It was a blunder that he knew he would never be able to recover from with Paxton. It was like he had erected a poorly built house on a weak foundation, and a flood washed it all away.

"Detective, are you okay?"

Shirley's raspy voice was recognizable without looking at her. She organized the container of sugars in front of him. Montoya was sure his face told the whole story.

"Fine, honey, thank you." He put a twenty-dollar bill down

on the table and headed out to his car. Montoya couldn't believe what had just happened. He stared at the airbag cover on the steering wheel until it felt like he was going to fall asleep.

"You damn rookie." The radio clattered and Montoya put the car into reverse. He spent the next several hours just cruising around the city. No calls came in for him. He couldn't recall how many hours upon days upon weeks he must have spent clearing his mind by driving around the city.

Some of the pimps and perps scattered into the hourly motels like meerkats when he drove by. The original gangsters just stayed on their corners, unperturbed by his presence. They knew when the heat was actually on.

He rubbed his eyes with his left hand and slid it down to his mouth, grasping his face like he was trying to force something out. That's when it came to him, unannounced and unexpected. From some part of his old, gray matter that he couldn't fathom still producing anything worthwhile.

Montoya pulled a U-turn and headed back to the eastern part of the city. In under ten minutes, he was parked in front of the old castle. He sat there for several minutes, formulating what his angle would be. The gate opened even though no car looked ready to emerge. Montoya watched and then took it as a signal. He cranked his car and pulled up the driveway to the porte-cochere on the side of the castle.

It had been a while since he visited the castle. There was a period of time when he was here almost weekly. The road base that made up the driveway crunched under his feet as he made his way to the front of the house. Having been away for so long, the castle now felt cold and ominous. Montoya knew the rooms behind windows, but couldn't get past how dark they looked. They peered at him like tribesmen gawk at a foreigner.

When Montoya came around the front of the castle, he was surprised to see someone standing there already. The man stood silently and expressionless. Then, Philip extended his arm and brought Montoya in for a hug.

"Uncle Robert, I had a feeling you were coming."

SIXTEEN

Don brooded over his phone as it rang for the second time without him answering. It was his office.

"Goddammit."

Answer it.

"Shut up."

He picked up the phone and called the number back. The receptionist transferred him to his boss.

"Paxton, where the hell you been?" Friedlander barked at him.

"Pretty sick today."

"I don't care how sick you are, we've got the call with Strohman at ten."

"I know. I'm ready for it, just going to have to conference in."

"You gotta be here, Paxton. Strohman sent over more documents that he wants to talk to us about."

"Cindy scanned them for me. I reviewed them already," he said tersely.

There was a pause before his boss continued. "Well, you've got it all covered, don't ya?"

"I wouldn't let you down." The line went dead and Don listened to the tone while he tapped his mouse on his desk.

Montoya.

Paxton slapped his hand down on the desk. "I know!" In a moment of lucidity, he realized that he was talking to himself. At the same time, he couldn't tell if it was really himself talking. There was an internal dialogue that had been growing in volume for some time. He pushed back from the desk and headed out of the room and down to the kitchen. He poured a glass of water and tried to gain control of his thoughts.

Montoya knows.

"Christ," he whispered as he set the glass of water into the sink. It shattered and he cursed the sink, the glass, the world.

After cleaning up the mess, he slipped down the face of the cabinets and rested on the kitchen floor. It felt like a world of thoughts were being unleashed on him. A once quiet mind raged with violent and obscene thoughts. Just about anything sparked his anger these days. He couldn't account for the change in his personality.

In the silence of his maniacal thoughts, he made out a creak from the basement. It sounded like a rusty door hinge. He narrowed his eyes and tensed, waiting for the sound to happen again. It did. Don shot up and bolted down the set of stairs to the basement. The sound came again. Something in the basement bedroom. The door to the bedroom was missing though. A relic removed by a prior owner. He moved warily into the room and stopped next to the bed they had squeezed in there. There was only one hinged door and it was to the tiny closet. Don stared at the door, his entire body coiled and waiting for something that he knew couldn't come. It was just his mind, his messed-up mind playing tricks on him.

The hair on the back of his neck sprung up. His arms sprouted goose bumps.

"Hello?"

The door to the closet slammed open all the way, hit the wall and then slammed shut ferociously.

"Holy shit!" Don's first step was misplaced and he almost tripped himself. He gained traction with the next step and shot out of the room. Expecting something to stop him, he raced up the stairs like a running back. There was no stopping until he yanked open the front door and made it outside. It felt like he made it to "base." He folded over at his waist and breathed heavily.

The house seemed to breathe with him. The whole world expanded and contracted. Something shuffled behind him and he saw a short man in an orange jumpsuit moving down the road, in the road. The man had his hands perched next to his hips. His face was filthy and his hair was matted. A shriek emanated from the basement and sounded strong enough to break the glass in the windows.

Don ran to the side of the house. The man in the orange suit paid no attention and didn't seem to hear the sound from the house. Don couldn't tell if any of the man's senses were in operating mode. To the contrary, every one of Don's senses was heightened. Decision-making ability was another story. He had no idea what to do. Whether to run back into the house to see what was happening or to run as far and fast as he could. All this resulted in a very normal human response. He froze.

Nothing else happened for a couple of minutes. That then turned to five, ten, and twenty minutes. He just stood there, trying to observe every part of the house at all times. Then, he did hear something. It was his phone. He ran up the steps to the front door and stopped with his hand gripping the door knob. Another ring and he was inside. He surveyed everything while he found the phone and answered it.

"Don?"

"Yes?"

"It's Faith."

"Oh, hi."

"Just hi? Are you okay?"

"Yes. Yep, fine."

"Well, we're on our way back. I'm going to try to make it most of the way. I feel good."

"Be safe."

"Hey, is everything okay with you? You seem awfully distracted."

"No, everything's fine. I was just outside, fixing some of the downspouts." He went to the stairs to the basement and peered down them cautiously. The phone shot a burst of static into his ear. "Damn!"

"What?"

"Did you hear that, on the phone? That static?"

"No, sounds clear to me."

He shook his head and held the phone out in front of his face. It looked normal. It had five bars. "Weird." Something compelled him to investigate the basement. Maybe someone or something had broken in. A raccoon? He had seen one around the front of the house before. It had dipped into the gutter before he could really make out its size.

"I need to go, honey."

"Really? Got something urgent?"

He shook his head and looked down at his arm. All of a sudden, something burned. A pair of red marks developed from his wrist to his elbow on his right arm. Terror choked back his attempt to scream.

"Don?" came Faith's voice. It was distant and only half existent to Don. He dropped the phone and ran his fingers over the marks. They weren't raised. They didn't have flaking skin around them, like he would have expected had someone scratched him. Instead, they were completely flat and looked like someone had taken a marker to draw two relatively straight lines on his arm. The burning increased in intensity and he went over to the kitchen sink, fully immersed in what he was doing. Completely shocked and completely ignorant of Faith's calls to him.

He ran cold water over the marks. It had no effect. "What the hell is this?" A new sensation developed, starting from his rib cage. It was a tightness, like the air around him was collapsing in. Scrambling for the front door again, he slid to a stop on the hardwood floor and reversed course to go grab his phone. When he picked it up, it seared his hand. Don reared back and looked at the phone with an innocent disbelief. Then, he ran back to the front door and out of the house. Out of the realm of pain and confusion. He couldn't hear Faith say that they'd be home in fourteen hours.

* * * * *

Montoya passed through the grand entryway and into the study where he knew Philip spent the majority of his time. The castle always unsettled him. It was small comfort that Philip was able to live in there. There was still something wrong with the place. Like it was alive and always watching. He knew better than to broach the subject with Philip. It was a beloved sanctuary to him.

The two were an odd couple, no doubt about that. Montoya was entirely centered in fact, science, and cold, hard reality. He could never see the things that Philip saw — or that he said he saw. To the contrary, Philip probably couldn't believe that the vast majority of the world would never see the same things as he did. The insights into other people's lives. The glimpses into another world of energy ranging from the beautiful to the terrible. That's largely why Philip rarely ventured out. As he told Montoya a long time ago, he knew the spirits in his castle and didn't much want to meet others.

"Jameson with a splash of Pepsi, right, Uncle Robert?"

"I'm predictable."

"Pleasantly set in your ways."

Montoya smiled at his nephew's graciousness. Well, adopted nephew.

"I've got to admit, Philip, I've come here for business."

It was Philip's turn to deliver a smile. The smile was knowing and understanding, all at the same time. Montoya always wondered at this man's maturity. Always wondered since he met him as a kid. It was like Philip knew everything that would happen in the future. Knew the next thousand steps the world would take as if he had set them out himself. It was tremendously comforting.

"I'm not sure you've allowed yourself a moment of pleasure in the last twenty years, Uncle. I didn't expect any less on this visit."

"Yes, well," Montoya stood up and swirled the liquid in his glass. Philip looked at him quizzically. "It's just that I've been sitting all day," he explained. When Philip didn't say anything, Montoya pressed on. "It's about the house."

"The house."

"Your old house. See, it's about the house but also the person who has moved into it. The family."

"Those two girls."

Montoya was beyond being surprised at the things Philip could know. He was also beyond asking "how."

"Yes, they're the ones I'm most concerned about."

"That has never changed." The two men enjoyed a warm break in the conversation. "Are you going to stay for long?"

"I have nowhere to go right now."

Philip groaned as he pushed out of his chair. "I'll start a fire for us then."

Montoya watched Philip as he went over to the fireplace and moved some logs into place. Philip's assistant, Bradley, came and received a message from his boss. Or, was it more appropriate to say master? Montoya wasn't sure.

"Uncle?"

Montoya's head lifted slightly. "Yes?"

"I think we're old enough to talk about something." Montoya felt himself tense. "In fact," Philip said while pivoting in his crouch, "I think we best talk about this because we are so old, and before we delve into this issue at my old house."

"What is it, Philip?" Montoya was getting way more than he had expected.

"We are not blood," he said with a poke of the fire growing around the logs. "So, how is it that you're my uncle?"

Oh, Lord, Montoya thought to himself. He tapped on the side of his glass and Bradley was almost instantaneously there with another full one.

"When you were a young boy, I think around nine years old, I got called to your school for an incident involving another boy."

"Patrick O'Brien..."

Montoya rubbed his chin. "You remember." Philip stopped stoking the fire and turned gingerly to rest on the fireplace and listen to Montoya.

"Of course I remember. That was one of the worst days of my life."

"Yes. Well, that was my second day on the police force. I responded to the school incident. While I was there investigating the scene of the incident and talking to the principal, I got the call about what happened at your house."

"I think I knew all of that." The fire crackled and spit an ember out against the screen. "I did, I knew you responded. What I've never known is why you became a part of my life."

Montoya knew it was likely a question, but it was one he wanted to avoid. So, he deflected. "There's one thing I've always wanted to know.

Philip looked at him, and Montoya knew that Philip's unresolved question still hung about them in the air. "What is it?"

"Was it an accident?"

"Patrick O'Brien?"

"Yes."

Philip shook his head. "I am outside of the statute of limitations, correct?" Montoya nodded and took another sip of the whiskey and Coke. It was a heavy pour, just like the last one. He started to feel warmth in his chest and fleetness in his mind.

"I put that pencil right where I was hoping it would go."

Montoya felt himself recoil a little into the chair. "Why?"

Philip raised himself while leaning on the wall around the fireplace. "That part I'd prefer not to get into. Too many bad memories. I'll just say that the young man had it coming to him, one way or another." Philip made his way back to his desk. The room was now filled with the heat and smell of the fireplace.

"Whatever happened to Mr. O'Brien?" Philip asked.

"Do you mean what happened to him when he got older?"

"No," Philip said curtly. "What happened to him on that day? I never saw him again."

"He lost that eye. If the pencil had gone much further, he likely would have died."

"I wouldn't have wanted that," Philip whispered.

"I hope not." Montoya set his glass on a side table and started to get up.

"Uncle, sit down." Montoya raised his eyebrows and stopped his ascent. "It does not add up. You had just started on the force and you felt bad for me? For what happened to me later that day?"

Montoya blinked tiredly and went into his own world of thought. It could happen any day now. Death circled overhead at his age. He had done his best to keep Philip isolated from the past. But he didn't feel like he could leave the past buried as old as he was.

"Oh, Philip." Montoya glanced at his empty glass. "We'll need a refill."

SEVENTEEN

Faith felt her eyes burning as she tried to stay focused on the dark highway in front of her. She was driving into a terrible storm. Her mom warned her about the storm before she left. It was a tendency of the elderly to be in tune with the weather around them and beyond. Despite knowing this, Faith adamantly refused to stay with them any longer.

She had tried to get in touch with Don on several occasions, but just got the same static coming out of her phone every time. Other people were able to call her, though. Her mom to check on her progress. A friend to ask them how they were holding up in the storm. Faith got the report from the friend that the storm was dropping water on them at a rate faster than they could bail out. Entire towns in the mountains around them were cut off. Some were washed away. The federal government was being called in because of the state of emergency.

Still, Faith pressed on. Something didn't let her contemplate other options. The black highway sped under her. The headlights of her car barely illuminated enough to see beyond a few feet in front of the car. The falling rain and the sky unleashing it seemed to gobble up any light cast by her headlights.

She looked into the rearview mirror and saw that the girls were asleep. Thankfully, because if they had been awake, Faith was pretty sure they would be freaking out.

Every few minutes Faith would hit a puddle of water and endure a moment of panic. There was nothing relaxed about this drive. Her fingers wrapped around the steering wheel and would have crushed anything of lesser density. Her shoulders screamed in pain from being squeezed forward for so long. The only thing that mitigated the circumstances was a passing sign, barely visible. Home was just over a hundred miles away.

* * * * *

This second time out, Don had little interest in going back to the house. When he was able to stop nursing his wounds for a minute, he noticed the clouds converging above him. They looked like giant oil spills quickly blotting out the remaining patches of blue sky.

A raindrop smacked the concrete sidewalk. Birds screeched by him on the way to some avian hideout. Dogs that had been barking suddenly stopped. Houses in the neighborhood were relatively close in proximity, so the cacophony of dog barks was a normal soundtrack to his days and nights. Now it was the sound of their silence that Don became aware of.

Without warning, a lightning bolt raced down from the sky and hit a tree on his neighbor's property. For several seconds, Don heard nothing but ringing. No thunder preceded the lightning strike, but he could feel it rumble above and all around him afterwards. There was a screech from his backyard. It sounded like air passing mightily through the choked throat of an animal. He ran to the fence and stood on the tips of his toes to look over. A raccoon was fighting a cat right on the place that he had buried that woman. The raccoon, nearly three times the size of the cat, jumped on its back and bit into the back of its head. Another lightning bolt shot from the blackened sky and illuminated everything around him in a scorched white. The raccoon let the cat loose, which just slumped to the ground. Then, the raccoon started digging in the soft dirt Don had just placed days ago.

This snapped Don out of it. "Hey, what the hell?" he cried out as he started to race back into the house. He cut through the kitchen and barely noticed that his phone was ringing. When he stepped into the backyard, it was like another world greeted him. Rain was coming down in sheets blown sideways every few seconds. He ran to where the raccoon was. It was still digging but stopped when he was just a few feet away. It hissed and crouched down into its back legs. Don took another step and the raccoon did not give. He had half expected the thing to run away as soon as it saw him. It appeared to have no intention of moving, let alone running away.

With the rain soaking him, Don decided the impasse could only be resolved one way. He ran to the tool shed in the backyard, hearing the raccoon hiss again as he moved. With a shovel in his hand he ran back over to the raccoon. Lighting crashed around him as he took a heroic swing and hit the raccoon with the back side of the shovel's blade. He was stunned that he connected with full force. That the raccoon didn't even try to get away. Its focus on digging down into that hole was so strong. The animal's body quivered for several seconds and then stopped. Don watched the raccoon expire as he leaned on his shovel, breathing heavily.

A door slammed, and then another. He spun around and could barely make out the top of Faith's car. He heard the scream of the girls as they ran for the front door. Don struggled with this new situation. He was barely removed from the chaos of killing the raccoon. There was a mini-pet cemetery around him now. He couldn't think of anything that would do him any good. So, he just started digging two new holes.

* * * * *

"On the count of three, I want you two to run for the house, okay?"

The girls nodded. They had been solemnly awake for the last thirty minutes of the drive. Faith's worried muttering woke them up. It could have been the sudden flashes of lightning. Either way, they woke up to a different and enraged world, and to a worried mother.

"One..." The roll of thunder almost drowned her voice out. "Two, three!" The girls opened their doors and slammed them as they made a straight line for the house. Faith jumped out and saw her phone sitting in the console. She looked at the girls through the windows of the car, reached back in and grabbed the phone. She put her hand over her head and started to run for the house. Just as she passed the back of the car, she heard a knocking from the window that faced the street. It was a second-story window. She slowed and looked up. There were another series of raps, loud but not quite bangs. Faith saw a pale face, almost translucent.

"Come on, Mom!" the girls cried out to her.

They were on the front stoop, waiting for her to open the door. She looked back at the window and there was nothing there so she hurried to the girls. Faith reached the door in a bluster. Shoving water off of her face, she searched for her keys. Brooke tried the handle and the door opened.

"That's weird," Faith said to them. They usually always kept the front door locked, even when home. "Don?" Faith called out while holding the girls back. There was no answer so she stepped through the doorway. Everything in the house seemed to be in order. The living room and kitchen lights were on. She could hear a television from the bedroom.

"Close the door, honey," she said to Charity. The storm was so forceful that she was afraid it would develop a form of its own and force itself into the house.

"Mama, where's Dad?" Charity asked while she complied. Brooke ran up the stairs to the bedroom level.

"He's not up here!" Faith started to head down the stairs to the garden level when she heard Brooke call out again. "He's outside!"

Outside? Faith thought. *Couldn't be, not in this.* She continued to the garden-level window with a view into the backyard. Sure enough, Don was out there. "Is that a shovel?" she asked the empty room.

Faith heard the patter of footsteps through the old floor above her. "Dad! Daaaaad!!" the girls screamed out. She watched Don as he remained focused on whatever he was doing. Maybe it was the violence of the storm that kept their voices from his ears. Maybe it was his focus. Either way, he kept digging.

She sighed and ran back up the stairs. The girls were perched on the threshold of the door to the backyard. Craning their necks to see Don, but rightfully unwilling to risk any of their bodies to the deluge, she nudged them aside, covered her head with her hoodie and ventured back outside. The rain and wind combined to almost force her back into the house. She struggled a step and then made it down another.

"Don?!" The storm grabbed her words and threw them into the ground. She ran down the patio to the lawn just in front of where Don was digging. "Don!" He turned around and they locked eyes. His looked rabid. He waved her off and went back to digging. Faith took the few steps over to him and grabbed his arm. Don shook her off forcefully.

"Let me finish!"

"What are you doing?!"

"Burying two bodies. What's it look like?" Water dripped down his face as he stopped digging and stared at her. "Get inside!"

Faith nodded and backed away without turning around. His eyes remained locked on her and a bolt of lightning crossed sideways through the sky before making its jagged descent to the earth. She headed back into the house and grabbed a towel from Charity.

"Thank you, sweetie."

After wiping herself down, Faith kicked her shoes off. Her teeth started chattering so she made her way up to their bedroom and changed into dry clothes. It was at that time she heard the girls scream for Don. She headed back downstairs, trying to fight off the fatigue of the drive and then this adrenaline rush. Don was in the kitchen drying himself off with the damp towel she had just used.

"Don," she said as she brushed a wet tangle of hair from her face, "what is going on?" Shedding his jacket, she could see that his face was pale. His lips were a bluish color. "You look terrible!"

"Thanks," he said while pulling off a shoe. "If I told you what

190

happened, there's no way you'd even believe me."

"Try me."

He smiled. "Okay. I was outside, looking at this storm just as it was starting. I heard something from the backyard. Something screaming." He stopped and thought about what he had just said. "No, it was more like something screeching, terribly."

"Oh, Daddy," Charity said as she stood by his side. He patted her on the head.

"I went to get a look over the fence and saw this, this raccoon fighting with a cat."

"What?"

"See, I told you there'd be no chance that you'd believe it."

"Fine, go on."

"Raccoon fighting a cat. And, believe me, I was just as startled as you. The thing pounced on the cat and killed it. Really violently. That's when I ran through the house to go and try to get it out of the yard. When I got out there, it wouldn't budge. Damn thing stood up to me. So, I headed to the shed and grabbed a shovel. Then, well, then I just about knocked its head off."

"Don!"

"Daddy!" Charity screamed.

"That's what happened. The bodies of those two animals are buried out there in the dirt."

191

Faith shook her head. "I can't believe it. You did all that, and in the middle of this storm!"

"I know," Don responded as he finished taking off his soaked outer layer.

"We aren't going to leave their bodies there though, right?"

Don stopped moving and gave her a nasty look. "What?"

"Well, dig the bodies up and put them in the trash. Better than having the girls play out there. Who knows what kind of animals that is going to attract into the yard." All of a sudden she could feel tension from Don.

"How about I just put some sod over it and we call it a day?" he asked.

She thought about the suggestion and also considered the state of their marriage. *This isn't a fight to pick*, she thought. "That's fine, honey. Just cover it up."

He nodded and they set about getting him into different clothes.

* * * * *

Montoya finished his next glass of whiskey before he even started talking. In the silence, he could hear what sounded like a terrible storm outside. The castle didn't let on that much was going on other than the rattling of windows with the thunder and lightning. The rest of the structure was constructed in a way that would never be replicated again, and would outlast the homes built around it by centuries.

His voice finally filled the small space between his lips. "Your mother did not die on that day." Philip, who was usually collected, tensed when Montoya said this. He didn't say anything, and Montoya knew it was incumbent on him to keep explaining. "She was going to die. She knew that just as well as anyone else. Your mother didn't want you to see her struggle. She didn't want you to see the end and go through again what you already thought you went through."

Philip sat up even straighter in his chair. Montoya saw him pull his shirt-sleeves taut beyond the edges of his sweater.

"My mother did not die on that day."

Montoya could not decipher whether it was a question or a restatement of what he had just said, so he remained silent. The fire continued to burn and crackle, happily irreverent.

"When did she die?"

"Eight days and fourteen hours after we responded to your house."

"Eight days and ... how do you know that so accurately?" Bradley appeared from another room. Nothing was in his hands. He was not there to offer them anything. It was then that Montoya realized just how connected the caretaker was to Philip. Even a hint of distress from Philip was loud like the doorbell throughout the house.

"Your mother meant a lot to me."

"You had known her for eight days and change. How much could she have meant to you?"

"A lot. Like I said."

"Did you know her from before? Before that day?" Philip shooed Bradley away.

Montoya sat forward in his deep chair. Philip sat to Montoya's right, almost perpendicular to him. He made eye contact with Philip. "I never knew her before, but those few days were enough for me to know what kind of person she was."

"I just . . . I can't believe that she never wanted to see me."

"That's wrong and selfish to say," Montoya snapped at Philip. "Of course she wanted to see you."

"Really?" Philip said with an almost boyish tone. "Then, why didn't she just reach out to me, even once? Even at the end? She thought she was doing something good for me by never making the effort?"

"She did do something good for you, Philip."

"I fail to see how that's true."

"She was completely paralyzed from the neck down after what your father did to her. She was confused and forgetful, likely from a concussion. Can you imagine your pain seeing your mother like that? If you had walked into the hospital room only to find that she didn't remember you? That she couldn't? Do you think that would really be better for you to experience at that age?"

"It's not right to be shielded from life, from what life has in store for us at every moment."

"You're naive, Philip. You've never had children, so I'm not sure how you could even understand the implications of letting them be exposed to something like that."

"You've never been through anything like this, so what would you know?" Philip retorted. At this moment, he seemed to catch the increasingly childish tone of his voice and responses. He also had no idea how wrong he was. They fell back into a discontent silence.

"What's this about you getting to know my mother?"

Montoya slid back into the chair. All hope of an early resolution to the conversation had vanished. "I spent nearly every hour of the day with her in those final eight days. She was terrified. Terrified of her state, of what would happen to you, of death. I could not, in good conscience, leave her to die alone."

"She had no family."

"None but you."

Montoya studied Philip and saw the creased edges around his eyes start to tremble. Slowly, Philip's body betrayed the tremors that started in his core. Montoya put his drink down and went over to hug him. This man he had taken under his careful and protective watch decades ago. As Philip shook in his arms, Montoya realized that his eyes had begun to tear as well. He shook his head at the beauty and tragedy of life. As old as he was, as many things as he had seen and experienced, he could still be surprised and overwhelmed by emotion. Philip nodded his head and Montoya released him.

"I'm sorry."

"Please," Montoya said.

"She died peacefully?"

Montoya went to warm his old bones by the fireplace. "Very. She was comfortable physically because of what the doctors gave her. She was at peace regarding you because of the promise I made."

Philip nodded again. "I suppose this talk was much more than you bargained for when you came over here."

Montoya laughed. "This was decades in the making. I'm just surprised we didn't talk about it sooner. I'm ashamed, too, that I didn't tell you earlier. I wanted to wait for the time you thought was right. It didn't seem like the thing to force." Montoya turned to Philip, his small smile still on his face. "But, like you said, I've never been through anything like this. So, I didn't have guidance other than my instinct." He knew that the tragedy of his own family was not something to reveal to Philip now, perhaps not ever.

"Uncle, I'm so sorry I said that."

Montoya waved the comment off. "It's nothing, and it was the truth." He walked back to Philip's desk and stood there with his hands clasped behind his back. "Besides, there's no room for hard feelings. This house, and the family there are what I'm focused on. I need your help."

Philip slid back from the edge of his chair. "Tell me, then, what is going on at my old house."

EIGHTEEN

Faith moved around the house tending to things that needed to be done. A lightness graced her footsteps. The girls were out on a walk with Don. She was able to blast some of her music and get a breather, however short. Plus, things had been great between her and Don since her return. He was making a real effort to do things for her, to tell her things that she liked to hear. They had even made love with Don displaying a mix of tender passion and aggression that she wasn't sure she'd ever seen from him before.

Scooping up a mountain of clothes, she made her way down the stairs to the main level by peeking around the pile and moving slowly. Faith readjusted the top of the pile with her chin and then headed for the stairs to the garden level. She took a step and felt something cold brush against the back of her right arm. She stopped and looked around. There was no sound of a door opening or closing. No indication that Don and the girls were back yet. She started to take her next step without looking down and her foot hit the edge of the step she was on. The moment came where disequilibrium started to win out against equilibrium. She dropped the clothes as she attempted to grasp the handrail. Her right hand missed, but her left hand caught a hold of it and she fell one step onto her knee.

"Dang it!" She stood up and rubbed her knee, assessing the damage that was done.

Faith gathered the clothes. This time she split them into two piles. As she delivered the piles to the washer she thought about the strange sensation on her arm right before she almost fell. There'd be no way for a draft to come into the house in that stairway. She pushed the button to start the first load of clothes. Right before the washer started emptying water into the clothes compartment, something rustled behind her. It wasn't close. It was almost like it came from the basement bedroom.

Faith stood motionless, hardly breathing as she waited for the sound again. It came.

"Brooke? Charity?"

There was no response. She edged to the basement bedroom and stole a look around the edge of the door.

"Girls?"

Still no response. Something scraped behind her, from the stairs heading up to the garden level.

"Girls?" she called out more loudly. "Don?"

Something responded this time. It sounded like a child's voice, but as if she was in an enormous aluminum room and the child was calling out from the far end of it. It was an echo of an echo. Faith made for the stairs and thought she caught a glance of something running up the next flight of stairs to the main level. She heard the patter of feet and picked up her pace, curiosity momentarily winning out over fear. There was nothing on the main level. Standing there, her ears were tuned to catch any sound at all. Her eyes darted about, trying to catch even a shadow of movement.

There was another sound. This time it was from above her. The attic. Faith heard a screech from outside the house and then laughter. She recognized it as Brooke's laugh. The curiosity of the sound from the attic was too strong, and Faith also wanted to figure out what it was before her girls got into the house. She ran up the short flight of stairs to the landing and stopped, looking up the last flight of stairs that carved back the other way. Nothing there. The front door opened and the alarm system beeped. Faith went up three more stairs and then stopped.

"Momma?" Charity called out. Just as Faith was about to answer, she heard a deep moan and cold air rushed past her. She tried to take a step back but missed and started to fall. This time, there was no catching herself. As she fell, she could swear that she saw a small, translucent face. She hit one step with the back of her head and the world went black.

* * * * *

Bradley brought in a plate of hors d'oeuvres for them and stood by silently. He was close enough to be quickly available, but far enough away to melt into the hallway. Montoya watched him and wondered where that man had come from. He also wondered how Bradley seemed to appear as ageless and structurally sound as the castle around them. Taking a bite of some cheese that Philip described with admiration, Montoya thought about the fact that his only primary cheese decision was medium or sharp cheddar.

"Yes, very good," he said after Philip stopped. An exquisite phonograph oozed Beethoven's Symphony No. 9. Again, the music was not necessarily lost on Montoya, but he was a Roy Orbison and Elvis Presley man. He lit a cigarette and tilted his head at Philip.

"You sure do lead a different life."

Philip smiled. He pushed his hands out toward Montoya. "Guilty!" His eyes glowed in the low light and reflected the dying embers of the fire. The grind of the phonograph's needle was audible when the men stopped talking.

"The people living in that old house of yours are in trouble." Philip's smile disappeared.

"Why do you say that?"

"My instinct. My gut tells me."

"No empirical evidence?"

Montoya shook his head. "None yet, really. There was a strange occurrence recently. A friend of the husband died in a freak accident behind the house. I'm also getting some abnormal reads on the husband."

Philip held his hand up. "You need to take a step back. Tell me at least something about the family."

Montoya's eyebrows flicked up and then settled back into their permanently contemplative look. "Family of four. Parents are probably in their early forties. Two daughters, twins. Public record shows that they purchased the house fourteen months ago."

"What happened to the prior owner?"

"Nothing of note. Nothing since your family has happened in that house."

"Did the prior owner have any children?"

201

"None."

"That would explain it."

"What do you mean?"

"It's the children they're interested in." Philip extended a small tin to Montoya, who rejected it. Philip opened it and pinched a bit of snuff out between his thumb and index finger. He inhaled quickly but gently and let out a long breath. "Impossible habit to get rid of." Montoya flashed his pack of cigarettes in accord.

"You said they?"

"Yes, well, it's just a presumption that I have. I'm fairly certain that there are several of them in that house."

"By them, you mean ghosts," Montoya said, almost reluctantly.

"Spirits. Most of them are probably just spirits. There is something more than just the spirits though." Montoya took a deep drag of his cigarette and let it out through both of his nostrils. "You know, I tried that once and I thought I would vomit."

That elicited a coughing laugh from Montoya. His free hand rubbed his eyes and drew down over his mouth. "You know that I do not believe in any of these spirit things?"

Philip took another pinch of snuff out of his tin. "After the things you've seen?" Philip's attention suddenly turned to

202

something else. "Bradley, the fire, please!" He turned back to Montoya, "It's getting cold in here. And, that storm, it continues on."

Bradley came into the sitting room with an armful of wood. His hair and face were wet.

"What's happening outside?" Montoya asked.

"A terrible storm," Bradley answered. The caretaker's voice stopped Montoya in his tracks for a moment. He was half-expecting the answer to come from Philip, although he had directed it to Bradley.

"Everything all right?" Philip asked.

"Yes, sir," Bradley answered before melting back into the walls and leaving the two to their prior conversation.

"Here's the problem with me believing in any of that," Montoya started. "If I believed, then I would have to believe that there's something else that can control a man or woman to commit crimes. It is plain and simple. How could I account for their crimes if they are compelled by something other than their own intent?"

Philip mulled this over. "I understand, but that means you have to completely ignore things you know to be true."

"No, Philip, I know nothing to be true except that man controls his every action. Every moment. If I attribute that to a spirit or a God . . ." he trailed off. "Then, I could not do my job."

Philip sat forward. The low light emanating from a small

203

lamp on his desk lit the left side of his face. "Uncle, what I am asking you is *different*. I understand the importance of your beliefs given your job. However, just because you believe something to make it align with your day on a practical level does not mean you actually *believe* the fiction you have created for yourself?"

Montoya winced at Philip's piercing logic.

"Do you believe in God, Uncle?"

"I do not."

"Because of all the things you've seen."

"That, plus what I was just explaining to you."

Philip nodded his understanding. "There's something godless in that house. I know that may not have meaning to you, because you do not believe, but I have no other way to describe it. For the short time that I lived there, I remember being mortified at almost all times."

Montoya listened intently, his thoughts shifting between Philip's recollection and the fact that a family was currently living in that house.

"The force in that house was there before my father, I'm sure of that. It is something I have reflected on for decades, and by all accounts, my father was not always the monster he ended up becoming."

"All accounts?"

"Oh, yes, Uncle. I spent many years investigating my father's past through his friends and family. None knew him to be what he was at the end. None of them."

"So, if it was never your father . . ." Montoya rubbed his knees. "First, what I'm doing here is talking your language, okay? Assuming that ghosts and spirits and whatever actually exist, okay?" Philip shrugged his shoulders. "Assuming it wasn't your father who killed your mother and tried to kill you, and assuming that it's not your father who haunts that house, who is it?"

Philip stood up abruptly. He went over to one of the walls of bookshelves and honed in on a book with his finger. He returned to his desk and opened the book. Montoya studied what he was doing, and saw that the book was actually empty. There was a compartment in the middle of the book that had a bundle of photos.

"What's that?"

Philip ignored the question as he sorted the photographs and methodically laid them out on the desk. Montoya noticed that he kept one photograph and put it on his lap. Philip started turning photographs as he told the story.

"Here's the house, when it was first built in 1929. The builder was a man by the name of E.W. Guild." Philip pointed out a man in another photograph. "There, that is him."

"Okay," Montoya said, periodically looking up and seeing that Philip was very focused on the recount of this history.

"Mr. Guild built many houses in this area, as was normal in those times. From what I can tell after reviewing records, he built ten homes here. The first eight went fine. No problems, no concerns. You'll recognize the ninth house," Philip said while turning a photograph toward Montoya.

He studied momentarily. The house was almost a landmark in the area. "That's the mansion across the street."

"Yes," Philip responded. "That's where Mr. Guild's problems started. There were construction delays. Apparently, he could not keep workers on the job. They would just leave without telling him why. Because of the delays, he started to develop financial difficulties."

"You think this Mr. Guild is the one in the house?"

Philip leaned back and smiled. "Patience, Uncle. But, no, there's no way it is Mr. Guild."

"Ultimately, he did finish that mansion, which is named the Carter Mansion after the family that had it built." Philip turned another photograph. "That's my old house, the tenth one he built. By this time, Mr. Guild could not get any workers onto his project. He was running out of money, so payments to workers were always late, if they came at all. There was something more. Workers back in those days were desperate for work, so late payments alone would not have stopped them from working. They said something was changing in Mr. Guild. He was breaking down, resorted to drinking, and becoming violent."

"Hold on," Montoya interrupted. "How do you know all of this?"

"I have had a lot of time on my hands, Uncle. I made the investigation of the house the purpose of my life for many years, starting when I was in high school. Many of the workers were still alive during that time, and I tracked them down."

"I didn't know you had such excellent investigative skills, Philip," Montoya said warmly.

"Yes, well, there's no better impetus for investigation than personal tragedy." He paused, seemed to have a thought, but then let it go. "In short, Mr. Guild had to build the tenth house almost on his own. He had the help of one of his sons, but that son died sixteen months into the construction."

"How long did the construction take?"

"Over three years. Mr. Guild died just over a year after he finished construction."

"Labor of love."

"I believe it was more a labor of death."

Montoya flicked his tongue on the roof of his mouth. "You've got several more photos there."

"Yes." Philip turned a photograph. This is one of the house, once completed. "However, it sat vacant for thirteen months."

"That's a long time."

"It was, and it was a month later that Mr. Guild died."

"Any explanation for the length of time on the market?"

"That is murkier. Some say Mr. Guild priced it too high,

trying to make up for lost profits because of the Carter Mansion. But," Philip started while looking Montoya in his eyes, "some of the workers I spoke to said it was something more nefarious. That there was an unsettling feeling between both the Carter Mansion and Mr. Guild's last house."

"Okay."

"The man who purchased the tenth house was actually a pastor. Pastor Robert Hamilton Crewt. What he did with the house was this," Philip said, turning another photograph.

Montoya studied the photograph for several seconds. "Is that a casket?"

Philip nodded. "Not just a casket, but a funereal arrangement."

Montoya kept analyzing the photograph. He saw the chairs in front of the casket. He recognized the living room as the space he had been in when he questioned Mr. Paxton. His mind started to race.

"I don't quite understand. Why would a pastor be doing this in his own home?"

"You couldn't understand yet, Uncle. Pastor Crewt was here because he was run out of Ohio several months earlier. He was the pastor of a medium-sized church there. In all of my searches, I was only able to find one article in a newspaper that referenced his termination at the church because of 'lewd and obscene acts,' without any further detail."

"Without any further detail, meaning there was a whole lot

more."

"I would agree."

Montoya's cell phone rang. He struggled to get it out of a pocket he rarely reached into with his hardened hands. He looked at the device like it was a snake writhing in his hand. "Hello?" After grunting several times, he held the phone out in front of him again. "How do you turn this off?"

"It should do it on its own."

Montoya shoved the phone back into its pocket. "I need to leave."

"Right now?"

"Yes, right now. I just got a call from the station. You have one more photograph, though. What is it?"

Philip used his index and middle fingers to twirl the photograph around. "The only picture I have ever been able to find of Pastor Crewt."

Montoya was only going to pay the photograph brief attention, but it made him do a double-take. He cocked his head and leaned closer. "Is there something wrong with my eyes?"

"No. Not unless the three of us in this room share the same affliction," Philip answered. Montoya looked to his side and Bradley was standing there, unannounced and wholly silent. He started. "Where do you have to go so abruptly?" Philip asked.

"Why is that man all distorted in the photograph?" Montoya

209

kept nearing the image until he was able to see his breath condense on the surface of it. In the picture, there was an open casket with family standing around it. Everyone faced the camera. All wore mournful faces, save for the pastor's. He was not smiling, but there was something bright in his countenance.

"We have never been able to figure out a scientific basis for the distortion."

All the rest of the people photographed were clear as day. Montoya recognized certain aspects of the house, also very clear. It was just the pastor, and then just the edge of him that was oddly distorted. It was as if someone had shaken him while the picture was being taken.

"The pastor, Uncle. The pastor is the one still in that house."

Montoya took a breath that accounted for the last several seconds of short ones. "I need to leave." He turned and Bradley handed him his jacket.

"Where to, Uncle?"

He looked back as he headed to the front door and saw Bradley standing next to Philip's desk. He was holding and scrutinizing the photograph of the pastor. "To there," he responded, pointing to a picture of Philip's old house.

NINETEEN

"Faith?" Don yelled after he heard the heavy thud from upstairs. He was just taking his jacket off after having hung up the girls' jackets. There was no answer. There wasn't even any sound.

"Girls, stay here," he said with a hand on their shoulders. He ran up to the attic stairs and saw Faith lying on the landing, her body slumped against a wall. "Faith!" Steps were no obstacle as he essentially leaped to where she was and slid down to hold her head in his lap. She didn't respond. He slapped her face lightly and called out her name quietly. The girls were at the bottom of the stairs, looking up at him with wide eyes.

"Brooke, go get my phone. Call 9-1-1."

"Okay," she said.

"It's on the bed!"

He looked back down at Faith and saw no signs of life. Brooke ran out of their bedroom and up the stairs to hand him the phone.

"Hello, what's your location?"

"1108 Carter Road."

"What's your emergency?"

"We got home, and I heard a sound. A loud sound. My wife was lying on the steps. It looks like she's fallen."

"Is she breathing?"

"I'm sorry?" It was such a simple question, but something Don had not even thought to check.

"I'm sending an ambulance to your house, sir. Can you please check to see if she is breathing or has a pulse?"

"Yes, yes," he said as he put his fingers on her neck. He didn't think there was anything at first, but then he felt a pulse under his fingertips. "Yes! I feel a pulse."

"Now, is she breathing?"

He put his ear next to her nose and felt air come out. "Yes!"

"Okay. I want you to keep your wife immobile, even if she starts to wake up. Okay?"

"Yes, okay."

Faith's eyelids started to flutter and Don almost jumped up.

"She's moving!"

"That's good. Keep her still."

"Daddy, I hear the sirens!"

Sure enough, sirens were getting louder from down one of the streets. Faith groaned and her eyes opened to slits.

"Don . . ."

"Faith, I'm here. Stay calm, okay?"

"What happened?"

"I don't know, honey. We got home and heard a loud sound. We heard you falling." He wanted to squeeze her hard but the dispatcher's admonitions still rang in his ears.

"I fell."

"I know, honey." Charity started to cry and Brooke hugged her.

"The girls."

"They're okay. You just rest." A loud knock on the door drew all of their attention away from Faith momentarily. "Girls, will you get that?"

They ran to the front door. Don could hear them talk to the emergency responders. Next thing he knew, a whole troop of them were coming up the stairs.

"Sir, what's your name, please?" one of the firefighters asked. Don answered and continued to respond to their questions. He recounted coming into the house and hearing Faith fall. Then, he slid out from under her head as the responders started to perform their tests on her. They asked her to move her fingers and she did. They asked her to move her feet and there was a pause. Don watched her feet in growing apprehension.

"Faith?"

He looked into her eyes and saw a shadow of doubt race

across her pupils.

"Faith?"

Her left foot moved, almost imperceptibly, and Don sighed.

"Don't worry," one of the responders said. "After a fall like that it's not uncommon to have a slow response on movement.

Don heard the girls talking to someone and figured that one of the responders was occupying them. He recognized the voice though, even among the sounds and talk of all the other responders. It was an old, raspy voice. Moving to get a view of the living room, he saw Detective Montoya sitting with the girls.

"Hey! Hey, what are you doing here?"

Montoya stopped smiling and looked up at him. "Responding to an emergency call, Mr. Paxton."

Don checked on Faith and then headed to the living room. He got closer to Detective Montoya and hissed, "You know what I mean. You're a detective. What the hell are you doing responding to this call?"

"Daddy!" Charity chided him.

"Look, there's no need for you to be here. This isn't some excuse for you to check up on us."

Detective Montoya stood up. "Actually, it was." The old man smacked a cigarette from a pack and rolled it around in the tips of his fingers. "What happened to your wife, Mr. Paxton?"

Don cocked his head at him. They remained in a silent stare until Brooke broke it.

"She fell when we were gone!" Brooke fell back into a nervous silence. Even her courage was tested in this chaotic situation.

"Gone where, darling?"

"Hey, that's enough. You aren't going to question my daughters." Don held a hand out in the direction of the front door. He felt his other hand clench into a fist. "You can leave now."

Detective Montoya looked at his outstretched hand and then his clenched hand. "I'm not your enemy, Mr. Paxton," he said while starting for the front door. "I'm just trying to protect you and your family."

"Protect us? From what?"

They stood face-to-face at the front door. Don saw the detective look back into the living room to make sure the girls were out of earshot.

The detective put a surprisingly strong finger into his chest and said, "From you."

TWENTY

Montoya was driving around when he got another call. Dispatch wanted him out to a car accident with a fatality. He didn't get the good ones anymore. He knew it. They were nice about it, but they gave him the real crap. The ones that his partner — that junior detective with a head full of meat — scoffed at.

He responded to the scene of the accident and looked out of his window for several minutes. He didn't want to get out and put those damn cones and numbered tags down. Didn't want to direct the collection of any evidence. It was obviously just a car accident, a mistake. His mind was distinctly on other things.

Detective Grudowski was there. His partner watched him with a pen and pad of paper in his hands, surely thinking it was because of Montoya that he was stuck responding to this kind of stuff. He got out of the car and lit a cigarette.

"Too cold for you out here?" his partner asked with a distinct sarcasm. It was as sideways as a dolt could get.

"I was just studying the scene."

Grudowski snorted. "Not much to study." The car was burnt all to hell, including the driver. Grudowski was at least right in this assessment.

"Where are the occupants of the other car?"

"Gone already. Family of three. All of 'em had to be ambulanced over to the hospital."

"Goddammit." Montoya sucked on his cigarette a few times. "How old was the kid?"

"Seven."

"Goddammit."

"Kid's probably fine," Grudowski added. He knew how Montoya was with kids. They all knew. "Mom was the one that really took it. T-bone was on her side of the car, and all."

Montoya just shook his head. "You've got this handled?" Montoya couldn't see his partner shrug as he headed back to his car. He got back into the relative warmth. He didn't want to admit it, but it was too damn cold outside for his bones, as creaky and frail as they were.

The sun was starting its lazy descent, low on the horizon. He checked his watch and saw it was half-past four. His stomach groaned, urging him to a meal. That was another side effect of his age. Everything got pushed earlier. Waking up. First meal. Lunch. Dinner. There were about seventy frozen dinners waiting for him in his freezer.

Truth was, there was no way he could get his mind off of the Paxton family. He had that gut feeling that he would be called back to their house shortly. The overwhelming feeling that he was letting another Hassidy or Chen situation slip through his grasp. His phone didn't ring for the rest of the night, though. Later that night he fell asleep in his recliner, looking small among the cushions and the worn blanket that he pulled up to his shoulders.

* * * * *

"No, no, I'm sure she'll be okay. I don't think she needs to go to the hospital, right, honey?" Faith was standing at the kitchen counter. She shook her head. "See, she's doing just fine." The last responders looked like they wanted to get the heck out of Dodge. It was approaching dinnertime. "If I see any signs of *anything* strange, I'll call again, okay?" That was enough to push them out the door.

"Any nausea, lightheadedness, you call 9-1-1 again, okay, Mr. Paxton?"

Don nodded strenuously and escorted them out. He turned to Faith and watched her as she leaned on the counter.

"Faith, are you okay?"

Her face turned toward him. It was pale and ashen. "I saw something, Don."

He stopped moving in her direction. "What do you mean?"

The girls came running down from their room, where they had grabbed a sweater for Faith. Everyone stood silently for several beats in time.

"Girls, I need to talk to your dad." The girls' shoulders slumped in unison. "Go up to our room and watch a movie." Once they were out of earshot, Faith continued, "I saw *something*, right before I fell."

"Like a flash or something?" He was playing coy, to his detriment. It was readily apparent from her tone that she wasn't

218

talking about a simple flash.

"No, dammit, a *face!*" she said in a forced whisper.

"A face? Was someone else in the house?"

"It wasn't someone alive, Don." He might as well have been a wall that she was kicking. "You came in right as it happened. Did *you* see someone?" Without waiting for an answer that wasn't going to come anyway, she said, "I heard someone, too."

The hair on the back of Don's neck stood up. He didn't feel scared. It was more like he felt threatened and was responding to that.

"What did you hear?"

She stood up straight and pointed aggressively at the stairs. "A little child. Running up the stairs and calling out every time it got out of my sight."

"What did it say?"

Faith sighed and went to the living room couch to sit down. "I don't know. It wasn't anything I could make out."

He went over and sat next to her. His typical response would have been to hold her, comfort her. Instead, he sat awkwardly, knowing what he should do but being internally repressed. *Don't let her know. Not yet*, the voice said to him, springing up from the silence in his mind. *Don't affirm.* Don managed to control the yell that surged against the voice. The voice that was becoming more prevalent with each new occurrence in the house. They sat silently for a time before he broke it. "You hit your head pretty good, honey. I'm not sure how much . . ."

The words were empty and Faith quickly sliced through them. "This wasn't some illusion created by me hitting my head, Donald." She moved her body away from him. "Everything I saw was clear. Everything I heard was there. I didn't hit my head and imagine all of this."

"I believe you."

"I don't think you do," she retorted while standing up. "Let me ask you a question."

"Okay."

"Haven't *you* seen anything?"

Something rattled in his head, almost like a thought was dislodging. There was pressure. He could feel his body temperature start to rise. "No." It was the best response. No explanation. Just a simple "no."

Faith eyed him. "Remember the girls saying they saw that little boy around? Philip?"

"Before you all left for your trip."

"Yes. I think it was him."

Don headed to the kitchen for a glass of water. He had to do something or he was going to start sweating. "You need to keep your voice down. You know they're trying to hear everything."

"My voice *is* down," she said while trailing him.

220

"Don't get this crap back into their heads, okay? They seem perfectly fine and happy."

"You mean for the hour you just spent with them on a walk they seemed fine?"

Don curled his hand around the glass of water and squeezed hard. "Yeah, I can tell how my kids are doing, even from just an hour with them."

Faith sat down at the living room table and straightened out the tablecloth. "I need you to believe me on this one, Don," she said into the table. "I need your support. I'm not going crazy."

This time, he couldn't mitigate his response. "No one said you're going crazy, Faith. But, you are crazy if you get a concussion and then don't think that could be the source of the things you saw." He hated it. The irrationality she was demonstrating. *Why can't she ever think logically?* he thought. As he stood there thinking about his wife, he could hear blood flowing in his ears like thunder. She said something he missed as he stormed up to the room.

* * * * *

Montoya stirred from his sleep. He wiped some spittle off the side of his mouth and gradually opened his eyes. *Christ, it was morning.* The stress he harbored all day, every day regarding the Paxton household must have been getting to him as he now crashed at night. Thinking of them only brought back the facts and circumstances of Hassidy and Chen, which led him back to the tragedy of his own family. Apparently, a heavy heart made for deep sleep.

221

Sunlight tried to steal through his heavy curtains. The blanket on his body was still neatly tucked around him. It was as if some angel had turned him in and made sure he had the best night's sleep in decades. He hacked the phlegm out of his lungs for several seconds and then he knew it was all real. He was alive.

Nothing made any noise except the slow whir of his furnace and the tick of his old grandfather clock. Montoya's body ached in all the normal places, and his elbow clicked when he took the blanket off. He folded it neatly and put it on the back of the chair. While his body objected to starting the day, as it was wont to do, his mind had an unusual vigor to it. Sure, the sleep likely explained a part of it. However, Montoya also noted a vigor derived from clarity of purpose.

"I've got to get over to that house," he said as he pulled a cigarette out of a nearly empty pack. It crinkled as he did so, sending the still sweet smell of tobacco from the bottom of the pack up to his nose.

Montoya went through the familiar morning routines. A cold shower, something begun when he was in the army. He dried off his wrinkled body and looked at himself in the mirror. There was something different. He stood up a bit straighter. Purpose lifted him and his spine. It was enough to make him smile inside. He went to his closet and dressed in his usual khaki pants with a white undershirt and blue dress shirt. The cold outside was something his body and mind sensed, so he sorted through stacked sweaters until he found a navy blue one that seemed adequate.

Montoya did change one routine. He heated a bowl of oatmeal in the microwave. Typically, he had nothing for breakfast other than a coffee and a couple of cigarettes. His stomach growled though, so he acquiesced to its demands. After cleaning the bowl and putting it into the drying rack, he headed to his car and then to the Paxton's house.

It was all quiet around the house when he got there. He checked his watch and saw it was a quarter before seven. His parking spot gave him a vantage point of the garage door on the side of the house, as well as anyone who would come down the front steps. This time, though, he had parked far enough away that he wouldn't be so readily apparent to Mr. Paxton.

Montoya cracked his window and lit a cigarette. Behind a trail of smoke, he entered into a familiar trance of thought. The downtime present in his job could evolve anyone into quite a thinker. *Well, not Grudowski. All he ever wanted to do was talk,* Montoya thought. That was the worst combination, in his opinion. The intelligent people listened and thought. The idiots talked the most. Intelligence is quiet.

The garage door of the Paxton's house jerked and then started to open. Montoya rested calmly in his seat. He watched as Mrs. Paxton came out, looked around, and then the two girls followed her out. They were bundled up enough that their arms stuck out from their sides. He hadn't realized it was so cold. It made Montoya chuckle. Little kids killed him so.

The group walked down the street in his direction. He remained motionless except for his eyes. They still tracked like a leopard in a tree. Mrs. Paxton made a right-hand turn and they all started to walk away from him. There were two elementary schools in that direction. One was a public school. The other was Saint Francis, the school where Philip had gone.

The garage door remained open, and then Montoya saw exhaust fumes start from the car parked in there. The car backed out, waited for the garage door to close, and then sped off ahead of a white tail. Mr. Paxton was gone. Montoya checked the street that Mrs. Paxton had turned down with the girls and they were also out of sight. He lit his next cigarette with the dying ember of his last one. That was about the only time he felt bad about his decades-long habit. When he used a cigarette to light another. It was pretty revolting, even to him.

Time dragged by like the lazy singing voice of a blues singer. Montoya was adjusted to the life of a detective. Life consumed in fits and starts. A neighbor came out to gather a newspaper on their front walkway. She was old, a vestige of another time much like the newspaper she was collecting. She gave his car a long look. This was the type of person with nothing else to do than scrutinize the irregular.

Time passed, and Mrs. Paxton finally came into sight down the street. Montoya studied her as she approached. She wore her blond hair in a ponytail. It didn't look like she wore any makeup, but she was still pretty. Nothing extraordinary, but she'd be pleasant to both old or young eyes. She had on a pair of tight-fitting jeans and a black jacket with a fur-lined hood. Montoya saw a bird career down from a power line and swing behind Mrs. Paxton before darting away into a tree.

He waited until she got back into the house and then opened his car door. The January air dried out his eyes almost instantly. Traffic passed and he walked across the street to the front door of the Paxton house. A few swift knocks and he stood there with his hands behind his back. The thud of footsteps heralded her presence at the door.

"Yes?" came a voice even though the door didn't open. Montoya looked around before remembering the speakeasy opening. It was still shut, but he saw Mrs. Paxton looking at him through it.

"Mrs. Paxton?"

"Who are you?"

He held up his badge. "Detective Roberto Montoya. Can I get a few minutes of your time?"

She studied the badge and then his face. "What is this about?"

Montoya didn't have any expectation as to how Mrs. Paxton would respond to him at her front door, but she was proving to be slightly tough to crack. He paused, as he hadn't really thought about a response to this question, basic as it now seemed. So he responded truthfully, "Your family." He immediately regretted the word choice, as he saw her face tense. The last thing he wanted to do was start with something that would erode trust. "Everyone is fine. I just want to follow up on some conversations I have had with your husband." The lines disappeared from her face and he knew his immediate cleanup had been necessary. The door unlocked and she searched for a key to open the security door.

"I'm sorry, it's just that the neighborhood isn't always the safest."

"I understand. You're right to be careful."

She stopped before fully unlocking the door. "Sorry, but would you mind if I saw your badge again?" He pulled it back out and held it up again. "Okay, sorry, thank you."

Montoya walked in and stood in the entryway as she locked the door back up. She finished and directed him to a sofa in front of their fireplace.

"Would you like anything?"

"Yes, please. Do you have any coffee going?"

She looked a little put off at his acceptance of the offer. She corrected with a forced smile and went to the kitchen. Montoya studied framed pictures on the mantle. Five in total, each of them showing the girls.

"Twins?" he asked.

"Yes," she responded. A portion of a wall was in between them, so she raised her voice to talk. "Charity and Brooke."

"They're very pretty little girls."

Montoya didn't hear anything so he turned around. He was startled to see Mrs. Paxton standing so close to him. She had a cup of coffee in her hands.

"Well, that was fast," he said while taking the cup. "Thank you very much."

"Instant. It's all we drink here." She sat down in one of the chairs next to the sofa. "When we lived in Seattle, all we drank was the premium, five-dollars-a-cup brand. Part of moving here was an agreement to cut that out." Mrs. Paxton smiled with her next comment. "Drinking this stuff makes you want to quit."

He took a sip. "I don't know. Ignorance must be bliss, because I have only ever had bad coffee. So, this tastes just fine."

She laughed. "I'm not sure if I should be offended?" she asked with a raised eyebrow and a wry look on her face.

"Oh, please don't!" They looked at each other until Montoya knew the pleasantries were over. "It's about your husband, Mrs. Paxton."

"My husband? Is he all right?"

"Just fine," he said hesitantly. "Let me take a step back. And, I apologize for being so direct, but I'm concerned about your family."

She crossed her arms. "Concern over what?"

"I've been on the police force for forty-one years, and I have seen some terrible things in that time. I had two cases that stand out for me, even today. They were two cases I was involved in before the time the final acts were committed. I can't get them out of my head, just like I can't get it out of my head that something is going to happen here, to you all."

Faith smiled politely. "I'm sorry, but how does this connect to my family?"

"Forty years ago, there was a terrible murder in this house. A man named Benjamin Sturling apparently lost his mind and killed his wife. The Sturlings had a son who I took under my wing, with some help. For years, I demonized Mr. Sturling in my mind. I had seen what he did to his wife. I saw in his son the

227

ramifications of the murder. It wasn't until the two cases, the Chen and Hassidy cases, that I finally started to lose my anger at Mr. Sturling. I believe that because I saw those two men unravel, because I saw them lose all connection from right and wrong, that I began to understand what may have happened to Mr. Sturling." He stopped to shake his head, "I was so young when the Sturling murder took place in this house. What we miss in youth is thrown back in our face in old age."

"Mr. Montoya. Or, Detective?"

"You can just call me Robert."

"Robert, this has some connection to Don?"

"It does. I assume he told you about his friend being killed behind the house?"

"What? No."

"Steve Lischek, did you know him?"

"Oh my goodness, Steve? Are you serious?"

Montoya was surprised that Paxton hadn't told her. "Unfortunately, yes. I'm sorry," he said as he picked the cup of coffee back up. A fire truck went by the house and he stopped talking to let it pass. "I'm sorry. I thought you would have known."

"I had no idea. What happened?"

"It was a couple of weeks ago. I don't believe that I saw you here."

"You were here?"

"Yes. I was the detective called out to the incident." He took another sip of the coffee. It really was bad, even by the low standards of his desensitized taste buds. "It was a freak accident. A power line fell down in a bad storm. It electrocuted Mr. Lischek right next to his car."

"I can't believe it!" Montoya could tell the shock was genuine, so he said nothing. "Don didn't tell me anything."

Montoya waved the comment away, even though he agreed to a certain extent with her sentiment. "I'm sure he was just waiting for the right moment. You did just have a nasty fall."

Her face froze up. "How do you know about that?"

"I was here the day it happened. I heard the call over the scanner," he lied. The truth was that he received a call from dispatch because he told them he wanted to know anything that happened with them. He felt her apprehension and added, "I'll admit, I've been a bit obsessed with the well-being of your family, Faith."

"But, why? And, Steve Lisheck is dead?"

Again, he didn't say anything right away. He glanced up from the coffee. "When I responded to your house on that night, I came in to ask your husband some questions."

"Wait, you think he had something to do with it?" she gasped.

"No, no. It's just protocol. To ask him questions about what

229

he had seen, if anything. To ask him why Mr. Lischek was coming over. Things like that. Like I said before, it was a freak accident in my opinion."

"Thank goodness for that." Montoya could tell she regretted the words as soon as they came out. "You know what I mean. Not thank goodness that Steve died. I can't believe it!"

"I understand. Getting back to the connection, what I saw in your husband that night concerned me."

She shifted in the big chair. "What did you see? What do you mean by that?"

"I saw the same thing in him that I saw in the men from those two cases. He was evasive about you, the family. He was nervous and edgy, obviously hiding something." Faith's head dropped. Montoya watched her. "There's something going on with your husband, Faith. I feel it in my gut."

A few tears dropped down her cheeks. "Your gut?" she said through a couple of deep breaths. "That's my husband. I *know* him."

"I'm not trying to take anything away from you, Faith. You do know him better." There was a beep from the kitchen. Faith went in there and checked on something in the stove. Montoya waited to go on, because every bit of time he could study her was vital. She came back and sat down. "Have you seen anything strange or different in him lately?"

She hesitated before answering, just enough to be noticeable to Montoya. "No," she said with a shake of her head. "Nothing strange."

"You just came back from a trip?"

"Yes. How do you know that?"

"Oh, your girls were telling me when I was over here yesterday." He set his coffee down on the table. "Just a little vacation?"

Again, she paused as if calculating her response. Montoya noticed every hiccup in her actions. Reading people was his realm, his expertise. "I wouldn't call it a vacation, necessarily. We went to visit my parents."

"Ah, they're okay, I hope?"

"They're fine. They're how they always are." Montoya could tell this was an evasive answer, but it wasn't the thrust of his questioning.

"Why didn't Mr. Paxton go with you?"

"Don? He had to work." She took a sip of her own coffee. "Plus, he doesn't get along with my parents the greatest," she lied. Well, half-lie. He wasn't the fondest of her mother, so she went with that half of the story.

"I understand." Montoya was now getting nowhere with her. He could sense she was holding back, probably a lot. He didn't buy the story about her visiting her parents at all, given what little he had gathered from her and Don. He could push it, but likely wouldn't get any more information at this point. Particularly when inundating a person with new information, Montoya had learned to progress slowly. She stirred her coffee a bit impatiently and Montoya knew he was about to be asked to leave.

"Could I ask you for one more thing?"

Her spoon stopped. "Yes."

"I have a very close acquaintance, my nephew in fact, and I'd like for you to meet him."

"I'm not sure . . . why?"

Montoya stood up and brushed his arms. He could feel her stare. "He used to live in this house. There's some important information he could tell you about it."

"Well, why don't *you* tell me?"

Montoya looked at her and smiled. "I'm not the best messenger for the type of information he has. Philip, well, he has a specialty that not many other people do."

"Wait, Philip?"

"Yes, why?"

"He used to live here?"

Montoya could tell from her face that she regretted asking this follow-on question. "Yes. Is that important?"

She stood up abruptly. "No, sorry, it is just a bit strange." Montoya smiled again. His internal alarm blared. *Not the time or place*, he thought.

"Okay, well, take this," he said as he handed her a card. "Please contact me in a couple of days and let me know if you're willing to meet. It shouldn't take more than thirty minutes." She nodded and took the card. At the front door he turned around to look at her once more. She smiled politely and then her eyes darted to the floor. Montoya knew there was more there, a whole lot more.

* * * * *

Later that day, Faith decided to take a long walk around the neighborhood before meeting the girls at school. Her conversation with the detective continued to rattle around in her mind. She felt confined in the house after the meeting, and needed a long drag of fresh air to counter the feeling.

The problem was that it was bitterly cold outside. A foot of snow was predicted for their area in the next two days. Cold bursts of wind reaching forty miles per hour started hitting her the moment she stepped out of the front door. The streets were silent. All of the dried leaves that clattered down the roads a couple of months ago were gone. Everyone with somewhere to go was already there.

Faith focused on words said by her mother more than the detective's warning about Don. She kept going back to the comments made by her mom that she needed to use her abilities in this situation. *Get real,* Faith thought. Her mother thought Faith had some sort of godly power to see and hear spirits on another plane. All she had were some strange coincidences. Being a true believer in God, Faith never once thought that she could have power that verged on His.

The elbows of her jacket scraped on her sides as she walked. There was a purpose in her step. She wanted to expel stress. Expel the nervousness she felt about whether that detective was right. Her mind went to the girls and then to her marriage. *How can I protect both?* A car honked. Faith stopped and waited for traffic to pass before crossing the street. The school was just up to her left. She glanced at her watch and saw it was time to get the girls. During those last blocks, Faith committed herself to giving Don a chance. She committed herself to believing that Don was just stressed from work, as happened frequently. Most importantly, however, she committed herself to be vigilant over any changes in his conduct. If it ever came down to it, the girls were first.

TWENTY-ONE

Don got home to the girls sitting at the table with Faith.

"Just in time, Daddy!" Charity called out. She kicked her legs in delight under the table.

"Hi, honey." He felt good. It was a productive day at work. There hadn't been any strange incidents. His mind was calm and, most importantly, his own throughout the day. Getting home to the warm, clean house and a nice meal with his family only augmented his good feeling. He kissed Faith on her forehead and then went over to kiss the girls on their cheeks. "This looks delicious."

"Meatloaf with mashed potatoes," Faith answered with a warm smile. "I figured it would be nice to have a heavy, hot meal with the storm on its way."

He nodded and dug in. They talked about the girls' day at school. They talked about the impending storm. The girls reminded both of them that their birthdays were coming up, and that there still wasn't a dog in the family. Don was as comfortable as a man could be, with his stomach full, his body warm, and his family content. They put the girls to sleep after watching a couple of episodes of their favorite television show.

Faith curled up next to him in the bed. He put his arm around her. "You've been awfully quiet."

She curled up closer. "Get that way sometimes."

"You?" he asked, craning his head to get a lock on her eyes.

"I think you've been quiet about a week of our nine years together!"

She jabbed him in his side, eliciting a grunt. "Just things on my mind."

"Oh?" He waited for her to continue, but she just remained nestled on his body. "What things?" he finally asked.

"My dad. He doesn't have that much longer, Don."

"They've said that for years. He's fought it all off this long."

"I've got a feeling."

"One of those strange feelings you get where the hair stands on the back of your neck and all?" He was teasing her about something he knew was a sore spot. Particularly after she'd just seen her mother. Anytime Faith was around her mother, they talked about Faith's "gift" and it made her sore as all hell. He knew it and was exploiting it for a good laugh. She didn't laugh, though.

"No, Don," she said as she sat up. "I have a feeling because I know my dad."

"Come on, Faith," he said while he gently brushed hair away from her forehead. "It was just a joke."

She fell back down into his embrace. "I know, sorry. It's just that my mom wouldn't leave it alone."

"I figured."

They lay quietly until Faith spoke. "There was something else too. A detective came by." Don felt his stomach drop and his entire body tense. The rug was yanked out from under his good feelings. "Honey, how could you not tell me about Steve?"

He told her about Steve. Don could feel the rage emanate from his gut. "I . . ." He wasn't prepared with an explanation. "I was kinda waiting."

"Waiting? For what? One of your good friends dies in a freak accident like that behind our *house*? You need to tell me!"

He knew it was better to play the mistaken, forgetful husband in this scenario. Play to the pity. "I know. I'm sorry. It was just so weird, how it happened. Then you got back and had your fall. I honestly kind of forgot about it. Probably repressed it would be a better word."

"You can't do that, Don. You know it means you're just stuffing it down."

"Yeah."

"Will you pray for him at church on Sunday?"

"Yes, of course." He wanted to turn the conversation back to what he wanted to know. What happened to Steve wasn't remotely important to him, knowing now that Detective Montoya had been by. Don managed to divert the conversation as discreetly as a drunk frat boy in a strip club. "So, what did you talk about with that detective?"

"Not much. Just that he wanted to get a cup of coffee with me sometime, or something like that."

"Damn cups of coffee with that guy," Don let slip out. But, Faith wasn't paying much attention now. Once she got the notion of falling asleep into her head, a pounding drum couldn't stop her.

"Yeah," she mumbled.

Don let her go to sleep and found himself doing the same in short order. Several hours later he started and popped up to his elbow. His heart was racing. He couldn't remember what he was dreaming about, but felt like it was something terrible. Images kept racing through his mind. They were all tinted red or black. A body crumpled on the ground, its head turned almost all the way around. A crying baby being dropped into water and floating away into the darkness. A dog being put to sleep. A cow being branded. A woman yelling as a man chased her. Don shook his head to try to rid his mind of the images. They kept coming. His heart raced faster.

He looked down and saw Charity in the bed with them. In between him and Faith. There was a voice in his head. *Our time together is soon*, the voice oozed. Charity's body became less clear. Almost as if her features disappeared, making her look like a porcelain sculpture. Making her something not identifiable as his daughter. Something screamed inside of him. Something released its rage into him and he wanted to hurt Charity.

"Don! Don!!"

There was a slap across his face and he slowly raised his head to find Faith staring at him in horror. His hands were perched over Charity's body.

238

* * * * *

Faith was stirring a cup of coffee in the dimmed kitchen light when she heard Don pad down the stairs. He came up and gave her a kiss on the cheek and then went about preparing a bowl of cereal. She watched as he ate it casually. *Did he remember?* she wondered. *How could he not?*

"How did you sleep last night, honey?"

The crunching stopped. "Fine, I guess."

Faith tapped the spoon on the side of the cup and set it into the sink. She went and sat with him at the dining room table.

"You guess?" This time he didn't stop chewing. "What do you mean by that, honey?"

He pivoted his head to look at her, but finished chewing his bite. "I guess I mean that it wasn't an extraordinary night of sleep, but it wasn't bad either. What do you mean 'what do I mean?'"

"Well, I was just wondering."

"Sure, and I told you it was fine."

They sat silently except for the mastication of cereal in Don's mouth. Faith went to get up and wake the girls for school.

"Hold on," Don began. "Something I couldn't get out of my mind this morning. You're not going to *actually* meet with that detective, right?"

She *was* going to meet with him, but she was a terrible liar.

239

Faith held onto the banister. She felt sweat form between her palm and the metal. "No, I'm not, but why are you so concerned about it?"

Don put his bowl into the dishwasher. "I'm not concerned at all. I just don't trust that guy, especially after he went behind my back to talk to you."

"I don't think that's necessarily behind you . . ."

"Of course it is!" he snapped at her. There was no remorse in Don's eyes after responding like this. He just stared at her. "He couldn't get what he wants from me, so he is trying to go to *you*."

"What does he want, Don?"

The question obviously threw Don a bit. "The hell if I know."

"Hey, watch your language."

"Probably still sniffing around because of Steve's death."

"Speaking of Steve's death, have you thought about that along with all the other weird things that have happened since?"

"God, here we go. What the hell are you talking about?"

She lowered her voice to a forceful whisper. "I told you to watch how you talk."

"I'll talk how I want."

Faith hesitated to continue. Don never responded to her like this. Curiosity won out in the end because she wanted to hear his

240

response. "Steve's death, then that animal fight in the backyard you had to deal with. Then me seeing and hearing that little kid running through our house. Shoot, your mom getting out of here like her hair was on fire. Isn't that enough to at least give you pause?"

"So, a freak accident, a freak fight, and then a freak sighting, and your conclusion is that there's something freaky going on."

She decided to let his characterization of her seeing that child go without a response, in the hopes of getting more out of him. "Yes, exactly."

He answered as he brushed past her, "No, I think the first two were just that, freak accidents."

"Hold on." Don stopped on the first step to the bedrooms. "You didn't include what I saw in this house."

"Look, Faith, do you think something other than your God was responsible for making a power line fall and killing Steve?"

"*My* God?"

"Let's just cut to the chase. Do you think some force in this house was responsible for making two animals fight outside?"

"What do you mean *my* God?"

"Oh shit, Faith, you're the one always throwing God and faith into my face. It's been like a bitter pill I've had to swallow for years to be married to you." She recoiled from his words, but had nothing to say back. "So, answer my question," he went on. "Do you think that some *ghost* in this house is controlling these freakish occurrences outside? Does that sound all that reasonable to you?" She shook her head. "Okay, then. Stop letting that imagination run wild," he added as he headed to the bathroom.

They said nothing to each other for the rest of the morning, and Don left without saying goodbye. She felt a tear in her heart, but knew what she had to do. As soon as she had dropped off the girls, she called the detective's number on her cell phone.

"Yes?" a voice crackled.

"Detective Montoya?"

He coughed on the line and then said, "I'm glad you called."

TWENTY-TWO

Montoya didn't want to take Faith to one of his regular haunts. So he suggested a hip and clean neighborhood coffee shop. He regretted it almost as soon as he walked in. The crowd was young and bustling. People were cloistered in corners. The screens of their electronic devices dimly lit their faces. He was used to bad food, worse coffee, and even worse attitude. The menu was enough to confuse the hell out of him, so he just ordered a regular coffee.

Faith came in shortly after he had ordered and he waved her over. "Good morning, Faith."

"Hello, Detective."

"Can I get you anything?"

"No, no thank you. I'll start today on my own energy."

"Haven't had a morning in the last forty years without one of these," he said, holding up his cup of coffee. They took their seats.

Faith started right in, "I think you're right about Don."

"Oh, just one minute please, Faith." Montoya pointed to the door. "My nephew is coming in, and I don't want you to have to repeat anything."

Faith turned around to look at the door, and then turned back to him. "Who are they?"

Montoya stood up and shook Philips hand. He nodded to

Bradley, expecting him to leave after seeing Philip was attended to. Philip sat down next to Montoya, and then to Montoya's surprise, Bradley sat down next to Faith.

"I'm sorry . . . but, Philip . . ."

"Yes, Uncle?"

Faith obviously sensed the confusion. Philip held up a hand that had three gold rings on it. "I believe I should do the introductions."

"Sure, but why is Bradley sitting here?" Montoya asked.

"You see," Philip started while looking at Faith, "the introductions will not just be for your benefit. However, I am Philip Sturling. You are probably unaware of the history of the house you live in. My family lived there many years ago. This," he said, pointing to Bradley, "is Wilhelm Gustavsson."

"Wilhelm who?" Montoya asked. He looked at the man he had known only as Bradley, totally confused. Montoya glanced at Faith, and saw that she had the same, confused look as he did.

"No, I know the history of the house," Faith started with stilted words. "But, I thought you died?"

"Not so," Philip answered.

"Well, if the detective doesn't know who this Wilhelm is, then I don't feel comfortable with this. I really don't want to share these things with three total strangers. Especially where the strangers are strangers to each other." Faith went to get up, but Wilhelm gently put his hand on her shoulder.

244

"Mrs. Paxton, I would wish that you would stay," he said with a subtle German accent. After some consideration, Faith acquiesced.

"Well, I'm with Faith on this one," Montoya said. "I want to know who this man is, Philip." What he really felt like, though, was a cigarette to clear the fog.

Philip let out a long breath and looked at Montoya and then at Faith. "It is difficult to know where to start, because you both come here with different understandings." He tented his hands and held them to his nose for a few moments. "Mrs. Paxton, as I said, I used to live in your house. On April 14, 1961, my father basically killed my mother in that house. Then, he attempted to kill me by throwing himself and me out of the window on the second floor. The room in the attic, you obviously know it?"

"I've been in there a few times, but it's Don's office and he generally keeps the door closed."

"Yes, well, to a certain extent it was also my father's office. The things he did in there, as we ultimately found out though, were horrible." Montoya watched Philip with some concern. He knew what Mr. Sturling had done in that room. They ultimately tied the murders of three women to Mr. Sturling. But, he didn't think Faith needed to know that. Not right now and probably never. "In any event, I was nine years old when my father did this to our family. I did not die in the fall. Just my father did."

"The neighbor, Mrs. White, she told us the story of what had happened. She told us you died."

"Rose, yes. She probably thought I did. We never saw each

other again after that day."

"But, my daughters . . . they also said they played with someone." Faith tucked her hands under her arms. "They said they were playing with Philip. With you."

"That is not Philip," Wilhelm said.

"If there was a boy named Philip in the house — you — and you're alive, then who was that my girls said they saw?" Faith asked. Her voice quivered with the question.

Philip nodded. "Now, perhaps, the story converges and I can address both of you." Philip turned to him. "These parts will be new to you too, Uncle."

"I'm all old ears."

"Wilhelm and I live in a castle called the Richthofen Castle."

"I've seen it," Faith said. "On walks. I didn't know anyone lived there," she added.

"Yes, well, we do," Philip answered. "The castle used to house an orphanage, among a host of other things in its past. However, it was more of a recruiting ground than a sanctuary for orphans." Philip looked at Wilhelm with a softness in his eyes. He didn't want Wilhelm to feel cheated by minimizing how important the orphanage was to many of the children there. "It was both," he added.

"Recruiting for what?" Faith asked.

"I know this will be a bit strange to hear," Philip started with an almost ashamed tilt of his head. "Wilhelm's ancestors started a paranormal society almost five hundred years ago in Germany. It was and still is called Der Giester. The organization started in Germany but has spread to various parts of the world, and the castle is Der Giester's headquarters here."

"What did they want with you, a little boy?" Montoya asked, glossing over the organizational details to what he personally cared about most—Philip.

"In the past, we struggled to find a consistent source of members," Wilhelm jumped in. "Particularly here in your country, where religion has dominated society nearly since its inception, we found few true candidates. What we discovered, however, was that if we could reach children here before they were indoctrinated into the culture of religion, we had a better chance."

"Wait, I don't like the sound of all this," Faith said. "You were targeting children and trying to make them disbelieve in God?"

"No, Mrs. Paxton," Wilhelm responded. Montoya analyzed the man in an entirely different way now. For decades he had just been the caretaker of the castle and the orphanage that Philip was transferred to after his parents died. Montoya had hardly paid him an hour of attention in all of those years. Wilhelm had white hair, like the rest of the men at the table. His face was smooth and, strangely, looked much younger than either he or Philip. If Montoya was doing his impromptu math correctly though, Wilhelm had to be at least his age. Wilhelm was dressed in the typical caretaker's outfit that Montoya had seen him in for all these years. A pair of blue overalls with a pressed, white shirt underneath. Faith interrupted his visual inspection of Wilhelm.

247

"Well, if you aren't doing that, why did you care that they did not believe in God?"

"We ultimately have no opposition to what members believe in, Mrs. Paxton. They can be Christians, Buddhists, Muslims, or whatever else they may choose. They can be atheists. It is just nearly impossible to convince a person that what we search for, spirits, exist after they believe in a higher being. The two tend to become mutually exclusive," Wilhelm answered.

"You search for spirits?" Faith said with a wry smile and a glance at Montoya. He smiled at her, but it was a half-hearted smile. He was more confused than her, and felt silly bringing her into a situation he obviously knew so little about.

Philip and Wilhelm exchanged a glance. "We search for spirits to destroy them," Wilhelm said. Then, he corrected himself, "I am sorry. It is more accurate to say that we destroy spirits when we are called to help. We do not need to search for them anymore."

At this point, Montoya had little that he could even manage to say. He had always known Philip was involved or interested in ghosts and spirits. However, he had always thought it was more of a hobby; something Philip dabbled in.

"Destroy?" was all he managed to utter. The clatter of silverware and din of voices around him seemed to eviscerate his word. He was barely sure anyone else heard it.

"Destroy spirits?" Faith asked. "Isn't that called an exorcism? Isn't that what the church does?"

"That is exactly why Der Giester was formed, Mrs. Paxton,"

Philip responded. "To get an actual exorcism performed by the Catholic Church is a monumental task. It is almost unheard of these days. Yet, with the advent of a new age of technology that gives us glimpses into the spirit world, there are more and more cases where exorcisms are necessary."

"You can't do it unless you're a priest. I mean, you don't have the power."

"The power of God, you mean?" Wilhelm asked her.

"Yes, the power of God."

Wilhelm smiled and sat back in his chair. Montoya and Philip looked at each other. There was obvious concern for Montoya in Philip's eyes.

"The power of God is in everyone, Mrs. Paxton," Philip said with a look back at Montoya. "There is no monopoly on what the Catholic Church calls its Rite of Exorcism. The words spoken during the process are not trademarked. The power comes through the person performing it, not from the procedure used."

"Even the procedure used by the Catholic Church is not the answer in all cases," Wilhelm added. "We have centuries of experience in this field, and the Catholic Rite of Exorcism is but one tool."

"So," Montoya started, "why did you ask me if Faith and her family were believers when I first brought this up to you?"

"Belief and faith in the people we try to help are what matter to us. Belief that there are higher powers we can appeal to in a battle such as this," Philip answered. "Belief in practices or

249

procedures or rules is not belief, and those people are the ones who are lost. They are unable to be helped."

"*Ein betrug*, we call them in Germany," Wilhelm said. "A fraud. One who kneels but does not adhere to the lessons of their religion. One who prays for everyone to hear, but who acts in contradiction to their religion for everyone to see. We cannot help these people."

Faith stood up again. She looked at Montoya. "Well, this has been a big waste of time. I have a husband at home who I can't trust around my daughters, and I have started seeing things in my house. You bring me this?" she said, pointing to Philip and Wilhelm. "The German ghostbusters?"

"Faith, I had no idea myself. I thought Philip *would* be taking you to the Catholic church. Or, something like that. I'm not religious myself."

"Mrs. Paxton, please sit down," Philip said. "No plea to any church would help at this point. You have no physical evidence of any spiritual interference, correct?"

"I have a husband who looks at us with murderous intent, and things I have seen in the house."

Philip shook his head. "That's not nearly enough, Mrs. Paxton," Philip said softly. He gestured for her to sit back down, but she did not. Instead, all of the men watched helplessly as she started to leave. Philip stood up from the table. He called out in desperation. "When it is enough, Mrs. Paxton, there may be nothing left."

* * * * *

Faith got into her car and started crying as she put her keys in the ignition. She felt completely conned. There was something she thought she could trust about the old detective. Instead, it had all felt like an attack on her, and an attack on her religion.

"How stupid could you be!?" she yelled and slapped the steering wheel. She continued to berate herself on the way back to the house. She got there and almost hit the side of the house when she pulled in. Tears clouded her eyes. Raw emotions made her feel nauseous. All she wanted was to get inside and lay down on her bed.

She got out of the car and started to walk to the front door. Something knocked on the bedroom window above the garage and she screamed. She looked up and saw the pale face of a young boy again.

"No, no, my God, please no."

The garage door began to open, making her yell again. She took several steps back from her car. She looked up again and the boy's face was gone.

"Faith?"

She wiped tears from her eyes. "Don?" His voice was audible but the garage hadn't revealed his body yet. She remained tensed and was ready to make a run for her car. The garage finished opening and she saw Don standing there. "Don, what are you doing home?"

He looked sickly. "I didn't feel well at all, so I came home. Come on in, it's cold out there," he said with a casual gesture of his hand.

"Honey, I saw it again. That kid! The same one I saw going up the steps! I just saw him in the bedroom above us."

Don took a few steps toward her and pretended to look up at the window. "I didn't hear anything and I've been inside." He held his hand out. "You look pretty bad too. Let's go lay down together."

"No, Don. I really don't want to go in there. I really don't, it doesn't feel right."

He took a step and reached out for her with astonishing speed. The grasp on her arm was like a vise. She cried out.

"Get the fuck in here," he hissed and pulled her through the garage and into the house. The garage door closed noisily.

TWENTY-THREE

The men sat around the desk in Philip's office. They had already been there for a couple of hours, and they all looked old and beat. Philip felt especially old. He knew this was his mission. Decades of waiting for the right moment to return to his home were culminating now. His mission—forgive and free his father.

"Is there nothing we can do legally?" Wilhelm asked.

"Nothing," Montoya said. "I have no legal right to go into that house."

"What about the danger Mrs. Paxton is in?"

"Nothing is impending. I have no basis to believe her husband is a threat to her, at least not enough for probable cause to go in the house. To be honest," Montoya said as he flicked the ash of a cigarette into an ashtray, "if I go around that house anymore and Mr. Paxton reports me, I'll be in some hot water."

"It would be of little use, in any event," Philip said mournfully. "You saw how she left. What help could we be?"

"I have to say, I was in the same boat as her," Montoya said. "How could you hide this from me for so long, Philip?"

"It's our duty, Uncle."

Montoya, likely feeling the heaviness of the situation, said, "Well, can I still ask Wilhelm to get us drinks?" They all managed an abbreviated laugh.

"I can still perform that duty," Wilhelm said as he rose and headed out of the room. His moustache twitched with a smile as he walked past Montoya.

Philip started making an entry into his diary. The diaries he kept spanned back to when he was nine years old. Wilhelm recommended the practice as a way of dealing with the feelings surrounding his parents. It worked. Eventually, the diaries became much more than just about those emotions. They became tomes memorializing all of the work Philip had done for Der Giester. They contained the trials and tribulations of over a hundred exorcisms. His cursive filled the page in neat lines. Where his pen stopped, the paper sucked ink out into small blots.

Montoya asked him something, but Philip began to feel strange. A buzzing sensation started in the back of his head and traveled up to his occipital region. He could faintly hear Montoya still talking, but he was losing control of his own thoughts.

Philip held his hand up as his head sunk down to his chest. He barely heard Montoya calling out, "Philip? Philip?!" Something else became stronger in his mind. It was a feeling of despair. A woman's sobs. *Help, help me.* It was the sound of another person's voice in his head, as clear as if they were sitting in front of him. He felt his body shake. It was Wilhelm, but he couldn't respond. He didn't even want to. *Help me. Philip, help me.* He couldn't believe it. It had spoken his name. He focused all of his energy. *Who is this?* he asked. There was a period of time where the silence sounded as still and as long as the ocean. Then, a voice started like a moan and the final syllables ended in a blood-curdling scream. *She's with ussssssss.*

Philip snapped to the world around him. Wilhelm withdrew the smelling salts from his nose. "Oh, my God. She's under attack," Philip blurted out.

* * * * *

Don pulled her all the way up into the room. Philip's recent allusion to what took place here made this all the more terrifying. Don sat serenely by the door and checked his watch every so often.

"Don, what are you doing, honey?" He hadn't responded to her for the last hour. Every time he looked up at her, she felt as if he would never speak another word to her. His eyes were largely white. His pupils had shrunk to something disgusting-looking. Between the fear and his eyes, Faith wanted to throw up.

"I know you're here, honey. I know you're strong. I know you remember everything we've been through. Don, my love, can you hear me?" He didn't respond. Not even a flicker of his eyebrows or a twitch of his fingers. He sat there like a breathing stone. The only thing that made him react was if she moved. She wasn't bound, so she could move. The slightest change in her position, and he locked on to see what she was doing.

After another period of time, Don finally moved. He stood up and pulled his cell phone out of his pocket. Faith watched him in disbelief. She couldn't imagine that he would be making calls at a moment like this, in the state he appeared to be in.

"Yes, hello. This is Donald Paxton. I would like to speak to the teacher of my daughters."

His words were like a branding iron pushed against one of her butt cheeks. She started to scream but Don threw his hand up and her voice was taken away. Struggling to even breathe, Faith

255

tried to take a step toward him. She couldn't do that either.

"Okay, but please let my daughters know that they need to walk home from school today." A pause. "Yes, they can walk home. Thank you."

Faith watched as he hung up the phone and put it back into his pocket. He returned to his seated position but kept his eyes on her. Her eyes burned as she looked into his. The small pupils left in his eyes twitched as she watched them. Faith rolled onto her side and started to cry uncontrollably. The girls would be here shortly. She cried harder when she thought about them.

She closed her eyes and tried to slow her breathing. Her chest still heaved every few seconds. Concentrating on her breathing, she started to do something she hadn't done since she was a little kid. It was something she had promised herself never to do again after her mother found her out. Her breathing modulated. She started to enter a trance state as she focused entirely on her breathing and certain parts of her body. Finally, she ended up completely focused on all the thoughts in her head and eradicated what was running through there. There was nothing left, no physical sensations and no thoughts.

She imagined Philip's face. She imagined him looking at her, then talking to her. At first, the fantasy was stilted. It was forced and she was decades out of practice. However, the more she relaxed, the more Philip lived naturally in her mind. After another deep breath and slow exhale, he was present in her mind as if in-person.

Philip? she asked. He appeared confused. Apparently, this was not something he even knew he could participate in. She felt her emotions welling up again. *Help, help me.* His face altered expression with the words, so she knew it was getting through to him. *Help me. Philip, help me.* His lips moved and she got her first words from his side. *Who is this?* Apparently, just her voice was reaching him. Whether it was a product of her rustiness or Philip's first exposure to this process, their connection was weak.

She started to respond but suddenly felt a rush of cold over her body. Her mind became dark and cloudy. Philip's face became distorted and began to fade away. With a breath, she tried to enter a deeper state of relaxation but she could hardly take the breath. It was as if something pressed down on her chest. Faith next tried to exit her trance state, but couldn't do that either. She started to panic, and then she heard a terrifying voice.

She's with usssssss.

The sound was unlike anything she had heard before. Tinny and like an echo, but when the echo bounced, it was robust and rattled her body. Her scream coincided with the sound of the doorbell ringing. Her eyes snapped open and she looked around the room. Everything was as it had been before. Don was starting to get up.

"Don, you leave them alone!"

As he turned to go, Faith saw something strange come out of the base of his neck. It was a small light, circular, that began to spread as it came lower to the ground. Don left the room, but this light darkened and started to form a more definite shape around the edges. It grew quickly in height and Faith could see the face of a man. The transformation stopped and the thing before her flickered. Still semi-translucent, Faith could see objects in the room behind the figure. She started to get up to run for the stairs to the main level but she immediately heard a voice inside her head.

You sit down, you little bitch. Or, I'll turn your head right around on your shoulders.

She fell back down to the ground and knew the voice was from the ghost in front of her. Faith heard the sound of the girls' exuberance around their father. Then, she heard them greet someone else. She strained to hear what they were saying.

"Philip, what are you doing here?!" It was Charity's voice. This time, she didn't care what the ghost said. She made for the door but just two steps away, her body was yanked sideways and she was thrown into a wall.

Sit! came the same voice.

"I see Philip now," she heard Don say. "I'm sorry I ever doubted you girls."

"Daddy, is everything okay?" Brooke asked.

"Yes, of course. Now, go downstairs and play with Philip while Daddy finishes some work in his room."

Faith tried to scream out but her voice and mouth were constricted as before. The ghost came and sat directly in front of her. Don re-entered the room.

"The girls will be joining us, soon," he said solemnly.

Faith squirmed on the ground, trying to make her way over to him. She could hear more voices now. Most of it was like chatter. Others were strong and clear. The voice of the little boy was one of the clear ones.

We can play down here. Remember my doll?

The chatter surrounded the child's voice like white noise. Another voice, something rhythmic, was barely audible. Chanting. The room she was in started to drop in temperature and grow dark. The chanting voice quickly became stronger than all of the rest. On one of the walls in the room, Faith saw the bright outline of a small door. It started to open and caused a vacuum in the room that was almost strong enough to pull her along the floor. A black fog streamed into the room and the door closed.

Faith instantly felt dread. She started crying as terrible thoughts raced through her mind. Thoughts of death and depression. Of the delight it would be to just die. Of hoping that she could die with her girls. The thoughts were impossible to shake, like a leaden yoke around her neck.

Then, the doorbell rang. The chanting voice stopped. *Go,* was all it said in an old, gravelly voice. Don stood up again and left the room. The black fog started to move past her, taking shape as it did. Faith could only make out the formation of its feet and legs up to its knees before it, too, was out of the room.

There were several thuds in the house, as if the main power had just gone off and on. With the last thud, the house was entirely changed. The walls were black and dripping. Something immediately smelled strongly enough to cause Faith to gag. She heard chanting and wailing now, but from a group of people.

The pressure keeping her pinned down lessened. So did the constriction on her throat. Faith heard another set of voices now.

These were clearer. They seemed to be from this world, and they were also saying something in unison. The ghost in front of her remained there, but its shape was less defined. A warmth started to build in her. There was a small light, superimposed over both her eyes. Not out of need or want, but out of pure desire, she started praying. No words out of her mouth. Just deep breathing and thoughts in her head.

After several seconds of this, Faith opened her eyes to the gaping mouth of the ghost. It looked like it was trying to swallow her head. She remained calm and continued the prayer. Soon, the ghost was sucked by its back through the floor of the room. She heard steps pounding up the stairs. Her heart started to race faster, but her body was overcome with the warmth and light that had started infinitesimally in her eyes. The steps were Don's. He ran into the room, his face a mixture of anger and terror.

"Stop this *now, you bitch*!" he screamed. "Stop the praying!"

He came over to her and took her body in a bear hug, as if he was going to smother the life out of her. Just as he did, Faith felt a pulse of energy emit from her body. Her head pivoted backwards and then forward. She looked into Don's eyes and they had reverted to normal. In that brief moment, she smiled and he smiled.

He put his mouth close to her ear and whispered, "Oh, God, please end it. I can't stop it."

He pulled back and she saw his face and eyes start to lose their serenity. His grip on her started to tighten again. She nodded and grabbed his body, which for the moment was slightly limp. Faith took one step, then two, and had enough speed after several feet to lunge them both through the window of the room. There was no other option for her. She had to remove this danger from her daughters. Faith's eyes were closed as they fell to the concrete below.

Girls, I will always love you, she thought.

She heard Don say, "Me too."

TWENTY-FOUR

There was certainly an odd feeling as the three of them approached the house. All of the curtains were drawn. Montoya thought he heard a humming around the house. They climbed the steps to the front door and Montoya rang the doorbell. After hearing no response, Montoya tried the doorknob. It was unlocked. He withdrew his gun from its holster and glanced at Philip. He could hear his heart pounding in his chest. Every strand of Philip's salt-and-pepper hair was clear to him. He swore he could make out the curvature of each one.

"That will not do you much good," Philip said, pointing at the gun.

"It could. Could need it against Don Paxton."

"Ah."

"We ready?" he asked them.

"Wilhelm, are you ready?" Philip asked in turn.

"I am. Remember what I told you. Pastor Crewt harvested and collected spirits. He will use them against us. He will use our weaknesses against us, and he will know weaknesses that you may have forgotten yourself. Most importantly, the more you pay him attention, the more he will focus on just you." Wilhelm pulled a book out of his pocket and turned the gold-leafed pages to a place marked by a red ribbon. "When my reading stops, it means you must answer what I have said."

A part of Montoya wished the instructions would go on.

When Wilhem's voice rested, he knew the real work was set to begin. He pushed the door open and was immediately confronted by Don Paxton. In the moment that Montoya could see Paxton, he never would have recognized him. What stood out most were his eyes. They were almost all white save for a small dot of black in their centers.

"Get back!" he screamed. Montoya fixed the gun on Paxton but his figure was gone before anything could be done. The plan was to have Wilhelm move in first. That all changed when Paxton answered the door. Montoya slid in while pivoting to his right. There were three thuds, the power blinking each time, and then the house transformed around him. He froze, his hands shaking. Something pounded on a wall.

"Detective, move further in," he heard Wilhelm whisper in his ear. Wilhelm's voice was transformed too. Before it was quiet and had some hesitation. Now, it was firm, demanding, and in control.

Montoya took several steps forward and braced himself as he looked around the area that used to be the living room. There was no furniture in the room. Just rows of old wooden chairs with a pulpit facing them. Four heads snapped in his direction when he came into view. They stared at him, their mouths slowly moving up and down. He was able to connect the movement of their mouths to a low-level chanting that he could only hear when he held his breath.

"Lord, have mercy," Wilhelm belted out. The voice shocked Montoya to some of his senses. He looked over and saw Wilhelm knelt next to one of the wooden chairs, his right hand making a sign of the cross.

"Lord, have mercy," Montoya and Philip answered.

"Christ, have mercy." They responded again. The figures sitting on the chairs stopped moving their mouths and stared at Wilhelm.

"Lord, have mercy. Christ, hear us." He heard himself respond to all the cues. Wilhelm continued to sign the cross and then pulled out a small container of holy water. Two of the figures got up from their chairs and came over to inspect Wilhelm and the container.

"God, the Father in heaven." Something pounded the wall behind Montoya and he jumped again. The front door slammed shut. Philip went and knelt down behind Wilhelm and placed a hand on his shoulder.

"God, the Son, Redeemer of the world. God, the Holy Spirit. Holy Trinity, one God. Holy Mary, pray for us."

Montoya whispered the response, "Pray for us." The other two figures were now behind Wilhelm. There were two men and two women. All seemed entirely engrossed in the container — for good reason. Wilhelm unscrewed the cap of the container and stood up. He bowed ever so slightly to one of the figures and then violently made the sign of the cross with the container. The holy water flew out and through the figure.

"Holy Mother of God, Holy Mother of Virgins, St. Michael, St. Gabriel, St. Raphael." Montoya answered with "pray for us" to each invocation, but he could hardly keep up with Wilhelm's pace. The figures were visibly distressed now. Their mouths chattered. Wilhelm shot the next cascade of holy water over one of the women and this sent the two male figures into chaos. They both rose off the ground and spread their arms to the side. Their faces pulled back and unleashed hellish shrieks. Montoya stumbled to his side and looked up the stairs to the next level. Paxton stood there.

"Hey! Stop there, Paxton!" Paxton made for the stairs to the attic. His body was a blur, but his feet fell like concrete blocks on the floor.

A stench returned Montoya's attention to Wilhelm and Philip. The two female ghosts were right next to his face. "Oh, God," he choked out.

"All holy angels and archangels. All holy orders of blessed spirits," Wilhelm cried out. Montoya couldn't respond. The smell from the two figures in front of him almost knocked him out. They were each dripping something from their chins. They were saying something, chanting something again. It wasn't anything Montoya could decipher, but it made him feel lightheaded and drowsy.

"Montoya, answer!"

His eyes rolled to Wilhelm and Philip. Philip was being backed into a corner by the two male ghosts. The curtains to all of the windows flew open and Montoya saw other ghosts pressed against the panes.

"Pray for us," he muttered.

Wilhelm began again with his prayer. One of the ghosts in front of Montoya reached out and touched his face. He fell the rest of the way down to the floor under the light touch. Wilhelm came over to him and threw more holy water at the two women.

265

They spun around and shrieked at Wilhelm. He put his hand on one of their heads and Montoya watched in disbelief as the ghost shrunk from the feet up to her head. She disappeared into Wilhelm's hand.

There was pounding from the attic. Wilhelm put his hand on the other female ghost and her mouth opened wide. It was frozen agape. She disappeared into Wilhelm's hand also. Montoya heard the shattering of glass and then the scream of small girls.

"The girls," he whispered to himself. Wilhelm grabbed his elbow and lifted him to his feet. The old men looked at each other. Wilhelm's eyes were tender but strong. Nothing needed to be said. Philip led the way down the stairs to the garden level. Everything was black, just like upstairs. There were voices, but Montoya did not see any people.

He was sandwiched in between Philip and Wilhelm. He felt the sprinkle of holy water on the back of his neck. All of a sudden, Philip stopped and slowly turned around. Montoya started to bark at Philip.

"Hey, I think the girls are down the next level," he hissed. Philip continued to turn around very slowly. Montoya fell back into Wilhelm when he saw Philip's face. It was hers.

"Missie?" He wiped at his eyes with his hands. It had been so long since Montoya had seen Missie Sturling that he couldn't be sure this was her.

"Roberto, it's me." Her voice was soft and delicate. It was very different from the voice he heard in those hospital beds in the days before she died. There were other voices talking again. Fast this time and urgent. He felt something on his shoulder but didn't peel his eyes from Missie.

"Missie, what are you doing here?"

"I miss you, Roberto. I'm lonely and scared without you here."

Something grabbed his shoulder again but he shoved it off. "I'm lonely too, Missie. I want to be with you."

She extended a pale hand and said, "Take my hand, let's go."

Montoya started to extend his hand and the next thing he knew he was belly down on the floor. "Montoya, get out of there!" It was Wilhelm's voice. He turned his head to meet the voice and saw the face of a small child. It was a young boy. He immediately recognized it as a young Philip.

"Jesus," he uttered.

"Uncle, come with me and Mommy. We need you to help us get away from Daddy." The young Philip extended his hand. This time, Montoya felt terrified. He was lost in this world, unable to tell what was real. The floor started to feel warm and soft, like it would slowly wrap him up and take him down into an eternal, peaceful sleep.

He was flipped onto his back and he felt something extremely hot hit his forehead. He blinked and saw Wilhelm straddled over him. Something was glowing in Wilhelm's hand. Montoya couldn't make out what it was. It didn't look like anything he had seen before. Wilhelm slammed it onto Montoya's chest and he felt his throat bulge.

"By the power of Christ, I compel thee to release this man!"

Montoya gagged. He couldn't breathe. He started to thrash and then his throat jumped from side to side. A moment later, something sprang from his mouth and vanished into the ceiling.

"Get up, we need to continue," Wilhelm commanded without hesitation.

Montoya wanted to break down and give up, but the look in Wilhelm's eyes was ferocious. Philip knelt by the steps. The prayer coming out of his mouth was audible to Montoya. It was "Our Father."

"Philip, your mother was here," Montoya said. He was almost afraid to keep looking at Philip.

Philip stood up and said, "No, she wasn't."

Montoya didn't say anything else. He picked his gun up from the ground and holstered it. It didn't seem intelligent to have it out anymore, after what he'd just been through.

"What happened to me?" he asked Wilhelm.

"There's no time. We must proceed." With that, Wilhelm headed for the last set of stairs to the basement. Philip went next and then Montoya followed them.

The basement was surprisingly bright. The light didn't extend outside of the room. It stopped exactly at the boundaries created by the walls and the one set of stairs. The basement was long and rectangular, with the farthest part of the room in front of them as they entered the room. More chairs were set up here. They were neatly arranged, just like in the living room above them.

Montoya saw the two girls sitting at the far side of the room. They were facing the wall in front of them. There was a chair in between the girls. In that position was an old man. He looked directly at them. His face was serene, as if he were greeting three old friends who had returned from a trip. Montoya took a quick step with the intention of getting to the girls, but he was immediately stopped by Wilhelm's broad right arm.

"He's right, you should stay where you are," the old man said. He was dressed in a black suit with a white dress shirt on underneath. He looked as real and as part of this world as the men standing next to Montoya.

"Let those girls go," Montoya demanded.

The old man laughed. Long and yellow teeth made up way too much of his face. "They do not want to, Detective. Do you, girls?" The girls shook their heads without making any move to turn around. The man raised both of his hands, palms up. Wilhelm and Philip locked their jaws and their heads slowly tilted back until they were looking at the ceiling. Then, they started to rise off of the ground. The two men were suspended in the air.

"Jesus Christ," Montoya said. His forehead was sweaty and the room started to spin around him. The old man approached him now. There was no rush in his step at all. It was as if he had dominion over every physical aspect of the room. Montoya's despair dropped him to his knees.

"I am so happy they brought the atheist," the old man said once he got to Montoya. A smell accompanied him. Montoya had smelled it before. As recently as when he investigated the death of Steve Lischek. It was not something that would ever leave the hair of his nostrils. Burnt flesh. The old man's chin had whiskery white hairs. His eyes were coal black. A bony hand reached out and lifted Montoya's chin. "It joys me to see you here."

Montoya struggled to remain conscious. He didn't have this fight in him. He was an old, retired boxer being summoned back into the ring to fight the current champion. "Who are you?" he mustered.

The old man sat down on the floor so that they were eye-to-eye. Montoya hoped that the smell would fade away, but it only seemed to get worse when the man spoke. "Pastor Robert Hamilton Crewt, and you are in my place of worship."

Montoya coughed. "Ugly place."

This made Pastor Crewt laugh, but when he did his eyes glowed like embers and the walls shuddered. "This, this is why I am so happy to see you here."

"Me? Why me?"

"A member of my flock, returned to me. Do you think that gives joy only to *Him*?"

"How am I a member of your flock?" Montoya's hands and feet felt cold. He remained on his knees but had to sink back down onto his heels.

"How? You are a nonbeliever. You are a questioner. You have seen the horrors of humanity and you know what doubt that brings. You know that mankind is filled with more bad than good, and you have seen things happen that should not happen if there was a *He*." Every time Pastor Crewt referred to the "He," it was like he was trying to choke back vomit. "I know you are ready to die, but I want more from you than that."

"What are you talking about?"

"I want to be a creator and witness of your reincarnation. The people of this world need to hear my voice. All these people you have seen in my temple, they are my angels. I vest them with my power, and ensure that the people who still walk this planet know I am here every day. Unlike *Him*, I don't ask people to have faith without showing my face for thousands of years."

"The girls."

Pastor Crewt smiled. "Lovely girls."

"I want you to let them go."

"I don't think you want me to do that right now."

"No, if I agree, I want you to let them go."

"They are not mine to keep," Pastor Crewt said, matter-of-factly. "Not yet."

"Do you agree, then?"

"Consider it an executed contract."

"And, them," Montoya added, referring to Philip and Wilhelm.

Pastor Crewt lowered his head close to Montoya's. "I have no use for them. Not even Philip, who I tried to take so long ago. He has chosen his side, and look at what *believing* got them."

Montoya nodded. "One more."

Pastor Crewt's head pulled back. "Don't overestimate your value to me, Roberto."

"Missie. Missie Sturling. Let her go."

"She's not mine."

"But, I saw her here."

Pastor Crewt held up his right hand and tapped his thumb and ring finger together. "Magic."

"Okay, how do we do this?"

Pastor Crewt rose. His skin started to change, like a blush, but made more noticeable by how white his skin was and how red it was becoming. Hair, which before was dry and white, now started to become more robust and gain color back. All of the wrinkles on his face started to fill out and his skin smoothed out. The room suddenly brimmed with spirits, and the chanting that Montoya had heard off and on began again. It was almost deafening now.

Montoya felt as vulnerable as a child. "Will this hurt?" he asked.

Pastor Crewt extended his hand. "Never. Nothing will hurt ever again. My promise."

Montoya took the hand and was led to the far wall where the girls were seated. He looked at them as he passed. He could have sworn that one of them mouthed something to him. It was as if the words were tangible. They were beautiful and suddenly filled his heart with joy. He and Pastor Crewt kept walking, through the wall and into darkness.

TWENTY-FIVE

Detective Grudkowski stood before the massive entry doors. He heard the doorbell ring inside the castle. Shortly thereafter, a man came to the door. It didn't look like this man owned the castle. The clothes he wore were too plain. He looked more like a worker or a servant of the house.

"Detective Grudkowski, I presume?"

"Yeah, that's me." Grudkowski waited to be invited in, but the worker just stood there. "Well, I have documents. Montoya said they were to be delivered here. To a Philip?"

"Yes, I am his assistant." The man took the packet of documents.

"Hey, it seems kind of weird to all of us. Montoya leaving everything he had to those two little girls?"

"Why is that strange to you?"

Grudkoswki shrugged his shoulders. "I don't know, just that the guy had almost a million dollars tucked away. Damn miser, we always knew he saved, but nothing like that. Anyway, I mean he didn't even know those girls. What the hell is he doing giving it to them?"

The worker didn't respond immediately. Instead, it appeared that he was sizing Grudkowski up. Grudkowski started to get uneasy.

"Sometimes, Detective, the string that connects people to our heart is not all in one piece. However, when you put all of those pieces together in the correct order, the path to the heart is direct and evident."

Grudkowski had no idea what this guy was talking about. "Yeah, I guess."

"Have a good day, Detective." The worker started to close the door. As it slid shut, Grudkowski heard a squeal and saw twin girls run across a long hallway. One of them stopped and looked at him. Draped across her arm was a ragged doll with stitching on its stomach and only one eye. The last thing he saw before the door shut completely was her wry smile.

THE END

AFTERWORD

Thank you very much for reading *The Room*—hope you enjoyed it. I also hope it at least gave you some goose bumps! It was a true pleasure, as well as a labor of love, to finish this book while our baby girl came into this world and grew up (very quickly) to the ripe age of two. She'll probably never remember it, but this book is dedicated to her because of the mornings and nights I missed with her to write it.

On another note, don't you hate when you have to speculate whether there's going to be another in a series? Well, there is. And, it's likely going to be called *The Church*. At least, that's what's in my head at this point. So, stay tuned. In the meantime, go read the Cruz Marquez series (*Enemy in Blue*), where I started as an author several years ago!